BEFORE
—THE—
VULTURES
WAKE

A COLLECTION OF SHORT STORIES

W.R. PONDER

LUCIDBOOKS

To Sarah, the purest happiness I have ever known.

You are the inspiration behind every beautiful phrase, the face behind every loving character, the sunlight in every darkness, the root of all contentment. Given a thousand lifetimes with a million pens, I could only begin to tell of the great love I have for you.

TABLE OF CONTENTS

CHAPTER 1

PANE

The first sentence is always the hardest to write, Russell Prey thought. *There's just always so much pressure with it. Is it intriguing enough? Does it enthrall the imagination or captivate the attention? Will it draw my readers in or push them out?*

Just one sentence. This was all he needed—a single sapling of splendorous syllables to take root and vegetate inside the reader's mind. All the other stories had been written—every one except the premier piece. This was what had long eluded the once acclaimed author; this is what he desired above all else. And it all began with a single sentence. One sentence—just one little meaningful collection of assorted letters.

While it is undoubtedly the eventual goal of any writer to have a work published and celebrated, for the one-hit wonder Russell Prey, it was a burdensome and crippling triumph. In all honesty, he wore failure better. With success came expectations, and with expectations came certain disappointments, and with those disappointments came failure, heartbreak, and loneliness.

Victory had become his defeat.

He now sat alone at his pine desk, hunched over as if looking into his own coffin, the face of the clock behind him twitching, the rain outside sweating down his window anxiously awaiting his next words, the breath of the morning rhythmically fogging up the glass in front of him like a curious onlooker. They were all his companions. They were his critics. They were watching.

His hands shook anxiously as they rattled the keyboard to his computer. Success was the twinge in his wrist and the stammer in his thoughts. For each word written, two were erased. His fingers faltered, tripping over themselves, fumbling to get a finished sentence out of his mute mind.

Exhaling a sigh of disappointment, Russell reclined in his chair, his eyes searching in desperate attempt to find inspiration. He took a glance at the few precious pictures he kept amid the clutter of his desk, pictures taken primarily with his mother and sister, his father seemingly always working anytime a photographic moment presented itself. His eyes continued their search around the room, flitting over the decorations that clung to his wall. The homemade poster that once hung proudly at the Donn Angelos City Library, the first edition of his published work, tickets to a baseball game that his father and he never attended—all of these items reached out to him, but none reached into him. They were only the shadows of inspiring moments long passed.

Russell rose from his padded rolling chair, grabbing the lukewarm coffee that had, for the past hour, sat alone stewing in bitterness, and moved to the window. Perhaps something from the outside world would give him enough of an idea so that the writing process could begin to work its way through him.

Russell gazed upon the city of Donn Angelos. From where he lived, on the northeast side of town, he could see life in all its various forms. Ahead of the City Heights apartment complex, where he resided, lay the unfinished beginnings of a government housing project that was under construction prior to the recession and promptly halted soon after the funding was redirected. The lot was now an open-faced maze of brick and mortar where vagrants and drug addicts congregated in midnight revelries and dark dealings. Perhaps the first story in his book would be about one of them and the unfortunate situations they might encounter trapped within the corners of the labyrinth. It wouldn't have been the first time someone had lifted themselves to success off the back of their misfortunes.

Redirecting his eyes upward, Russell watched as an afternoon drizzle of various birds rose and fell along the cracked and crumbling perimeter of the Hotel Grand. Once the glistening gem of the city, the old abandoned hotel was now a visual representation of the squalor many families in the area were growing accustomed to. Russell couldn't help but see the irony that the former residence of many of Donn Angelos's finest patrons was now home to a storytelling of ravens, a cast of hawks, a murder of crows, and a wake of vultures— each, like rival gangs, claiming a different part of the building as their own. Perhaps he could write on the fabled tenth floor of that old nine-story building, or maybe tell a tale of a misfortunate soul who moves in, only to find some unspoken horror lurking within those walls.

To the east of his apartment complex sat a small, rain-soaked Catholic church, and beyond that rested one of the town's two mortuaries and the local cemetery, which had a nasty habit of flooding in weather more inclement than this. While the city of Donn Angelos was not very populated, the death rate had always been abnormally high, an unfortunate truth known throughout the mid-Florida region ever since the town was founded. Any time Russell was asked why he chose to write horror fiction, he always replied that it was the genre that most astutely depicted the town where he was born and raised.

Looking directly across the way from his apartment, situated on the lowest of seven levels, Russell watched some of the community children at play in the rain, trooping around into the yards of neighborly strangers on a quest for entertainment and adventure, splashing through puddles, and kicking mud onto mean Ms. McKennan's doorstep. He listened to the sound of the tenants above him, layers of stomping, shouting, and thumping bass all funneling down into his living room.

He saw the newlywed couple from down the hall snuggle under an umbrella as they sauntered along the winding concrete sidewalk. He watched the orange tabby cat that belonged to the chain-smoking pregnant woman who lived above him make its way through his tiny garden and squat in generous fashion to provide him with free fertilizer for the next week and a half.

Now maybe there's the real story, Russell thought. *In a moment of poetic justice, a cat is eaten by the very same tomatoes that it levels with feces.* He smiled to himself. *Then again, maybe not. It would probably be a pretty crappy story.* Russell couldn't help but laugh; his favorite jokes were always his own.

With the devilish grin still lingering on his lips, there was a sudden crash in the living room.

An unknown object had pelted his window. Slivers of shattered glass littered the beige carpet under him as web-like cracks rippled throughout the enduring portion of the pane.

"Damn kids!" Russell shouted as he ran out the front door into the rain, shaking his dripping fists at the miniature monsters collecting across the lawn. "Who did this?" he bellowed out. "Which one of you little punks broke my window?" At this, the apartment children, or Heighties as the locals had taken to calling them, began to scatter, each to their own dry, safe haven, like cockroaches panicking to evade the light.

With his face still hot with anger, Russell stooped down, taking a moment to examine the object that had so forcibly shattered both his window and his concentration. It was a vulture chick lying on the grass by the window. Its head appeared to have a wet, rubbery black texture, and its eyes were strained shut. Its small, damp, white down-covered body gently expanded with shallow breaths, causing the tiny shards of glass in his feathers to reflect the outdoor light.

Oh my, Russell thought as both hands reached down to cup the bird's tiny broken body, *this changes things*. Somehow, the world looked different now.

He brought the bird inside and, after one-handedly constructing a makeshift bed out of tissues on the kitchen counter, he laid the pitiable creature down. Suddenly he felt a certain ownership over the fowl's fate. Sympathy washed over him like a warm and unexpected bath. Although he was no doctor, veterinarian, or avid pet owner, he knew that the bird's beak was smashed and one side of its body had been completely crushed by the impact. Helplessly, he watched the baby chick's breathing slow until its body heaved no longer.

Pity, sadness, frustration, confusion, and compassion joined him for a seat on his plush beige kitchen stool. A life—no matter how small that life might be—was precious. He knew he wouldn't cry; this was never a matter really in question. No, what he felt was less of a sorrow and more of a feeling of loss. As Russell sat quietly, processing the unexpected turn of events, he noticed that life, at least for that infinitesimal fraction of time, was moving a bit slower than usual. He saw the blood that had softly pooled into the tissue cradle begin to brown, before hearing the breeze whistle through his fractured window.

Wait a minute, he thought, *the window*!

The bird was gone—there was nothing he could do about that now—but his window problem was very much alive and well.

Russell reached into his pocket and grabbed his phone when he realized his hands had been sullied with crimson spill. Quickly washing the chick's life off of him, he looked up the nearest repairman to mend the mess that had assembled as an impromptu Pollock painting on his discolored carpet. Then he returned his attention to disposing of the body.

You have become quite the nuisance, my fine-feathered friend, he thought. As Russell reached for the sides of the tissue cot, there was a knock at the door.

Stunned, he looked at his watch. "Now that's impressive," he said as he moved to the front door. "I didn't expect you guys to come out this way so soon!" he called out a little louder as he turned the handle.

"That's always a nice—"

The heavy wood door creaked open, and Russell's mouth closed as he beheld the dark figure planted amongst the muck and mire. A cold, rain-wrought breeze smacked Russell against the cheek as goose bumps formed along his body.

"A nice surprise?" the man at the door answered through the overcast gloom with a crooked smile, revealing teeth like tattered tombstones protruding out of a pink terrain. "I can promise that we are full of surprises, Mr. Prey."

It wasn't the figure of the guest that rattled the writer into wordlessness. The man appeared a physical parody of a repairman, the kind one might see in a trite Hollywood movie. The man was both chubby and stubby, with an oblong head that sported long white hairs along its perimeter. His drenched and muddy outerwear was parted by a metallic zipper down to his chest, revealing an undershirt that was thoroughly stained with rain, sweat, stink, and oil.

No, it wasn't the figure of the man that caused Russell to feel displaced in his skin.

It was the man's eyes.

Something was very wrong with one of his watcher's watchers. Both eyes were sunken into the man's head at a slightly skewed angle, like the eyes of a vulture perched hungrily in a branch high above its next meal. One was a soulless pale blue, the other an intense, discolored, gangrenous yellow. It was as if God had tried to put two men into one body and given each their own eye as a souvenir.

Repulsive yet inviting, the eyes were a fearsome and curious sight to behold. Taken together they were simultaneously enchanting and terrifying, reassuring yet unsettling. And no matter how much Russell longed to preoccupy his mind with the tame blue, it was the embittered, infected, tawny eye that kept his gaze.

"I appreciate you coming so quickly," Russell forced himself to say, still watching the yellow eye.

"Yeah, well, we try our best around here. Especially for a local celebrity!" the man said, extending his hand.

As they shook, Russell felt the deep, blackened stains chiseled into the cracks of the man's rough and callous hands. No sooner had they touched then the writer was drawn back into staring into the yellow flame that flickered before him.

"It's a real pleasure to meet you, Mr. Prey," the man said leaning in closer while pulling Russell slightly in toward himself and into the rain. "I'm a big fan of your work."

"Thanks," Russell mumbled as he forced a smile to cover the palpable discomfort that crept over him. "Always nice to meet a fan." He pulled his hand out of his visitor's greasy clasp and jammed it into his pocket to avoid any future physical contact. He noticed then a faded red patch sewn onto the upper left side of the man's worn-out charcoal jumpsuit. *Mr. E*, it read. It seemed the eye on his welcome mat had a name.

"Where's the damage?" Mr. E asked.

"Oh, it's this way," Russell said as he led his guest from the doorway of his apartment to the scene of the accident. "It was the damnedest thing. I was doing some work at my desk when a bird flew right into my window here and smashed the glass all to hell."

"Yeah, those pesky things have been known to fly into any damn thing they put their little bird brain to. Like that movie with the birds. You ever see that? The movie with the birds where they were smashing into every damn thing all over God's green earth." At this, Mr. E paused in midsentence and, with a puzzled expression, began to scratch his head. "Now, what was the name of that movie? You know—the one with all those birds?"

"*The Birds*?" Russell responded, semi-sarcastically.

"Bingo! That's it. That's the one." Mr. E pointed one of his long fingers in Russell's direction. "I knew a smart guy like you woulda guessed it."

The yellow eye looked pleased.

"Right . . . well, this is it," Russell said gesturing to the window.

"Okay, okay. Let's see what we got here." Mr. E surveyed the scene. "Yup, yup. Just like I figured. I'm afraid you're gonna need a new window."

Unable to tell if his guest was joking, Russell nodded his head in agreement. "And you can do that, right?"

"Oh yeah—most definitely, most definitely. We'll get this thing knocked out and fixed right up in a jiffy. Shouldn't take but an hour or so to clean up and install."

"Okay. Wow. Great," said Russell as he silently thanked the gods of window installation. "That's great news. I guess I'll leave you to it then."

Russell returned to his desk and proceeded to pretend to write. He figured that if he looked busy enough he would be left alone and not have to talk to the stranger occupying his living room, an act which, he feared, would inevitably lead to more involuntary ogling. Clacking the keyboard one letter at a time, Russell's attention slowly faded, the nuanced typing rhythmically carrying him in and out of deep thought.

Afraid that the slightest pause in typing would be mistaken as an invitation for company, Russell typed his mind onto the page, all the while trying to conjure up the plot for what would be his next masterpiece. Everyone had a deadline, and Mr. Prey's was fast approaching. But what originated as a thinking project took an unforeseen turn when unwanted images of the yellow eye began populating his thoughts, turning his daydream into a nightmarish vision. The more he thought about it, the more it disturbed him. What was at first a striking feature was now a feature Russell wanted to strike completely from his memory.

Russell's imagination ran rampant, pondering under what condition the eye became so deformed. It unnerved him; its rotten milk complexion was maddening. The more he dwelled on it, the more he could taste and smell the rancid, vomit-stained eye in the next room.

Hearing his living room window pop out of place jolted Russell from his self-induced hypnosis. Stretching back in his chair, he looked around the room before focusing again on his document. Selecting the elongated paragraph of gibberish, Russell's finger hovered over the delete option when he noticed something peculiar in what he had been subconsciously writing.

Directly in the middle of the confused jumble and randomly assorted letterings lay a message that penetrated Russell to his innermost being: *theEyewillEndYou.*

At first Russell glanced over the hidden warning, but once visible there was no getting its meaning out of his memory.

The eye will end you.

Russell leaned in closer to his computer monitor and, in the stillness of the moment, weighed the likelihood of the foretelling being purely coincidence or something far more sinister.

"Mr. Prey?"

Russell jumped and jammed his finger into the delete button, erasing all evidence of the message. Looking up, he saw Mr. E standing on the opposite end of the desk, hammer in hand, yellow eye fixed on him.

"Mr. Prey—excuse me. I don't mean to hold up the works here, but I need to talk to you for a second."

"Sure. Right. Okay." Russell tried to control his breathing.

"You see, I need to run to my office really quick and pick you up a new window. I measured it all off, so now all I got to do is run out and pick up the right size window to install."

"All right. Do what you need to do. I will be here," Russell said flinching a fake smile, his heart still racing within him. Hoping his short, choppy responses were enough to secure the do-not-disturb impression he was trying to convey, Russell's fingers again began to type.

"Wait a minute! Wait one gosh darn minute." Mr. E pointed the hammer at the writer. "Are you writing something?"

"Well, you know," Russell replied with a shrug of his shoulders, "just some . . . thoughts."

"Oh my goodness. Oh my goodness! I can't believe it! Man, this is like a dream come true for me! Seeing my favorite author sitting there, writing! My wife won't believe that I was here today with you. Hell—I can't believe it myself! You know, she and me sometimes got almost like this language barrier between us, you know, but your book is one of the few things in this world that we both just love. Even when we got nothing else to say to each other, I just bring up your book, and she starts rattling off like a dadgum bird in a cage."

Perhaps Russell had impatiently misjudged his visitor. After all, the repairman couldn't be all that bad if he had read his book. "It's always nice to meet a reader," Russell replied, still doing his best to look around the man's face, rather than at it.

"I have so many questions for you—so many things that I want to say! Your last book was so good. And I'm not just saying that, you know. I know I don't look it, but I don't usually read too many books—but I sure read yours, and I don't think I put it down until I was done with it! Man, oh man . . . even just thinking of it gives me chills! The story was just so good! How the therapist was in love with one of his patients, but he couldn't get his wife to divorce him so he could marry her, but he didn't love his wife anymore, so he hypnotized one of his other patients to murder his wife for him! Genius! Where do you even come up with that stuff? And how many of the people's names meant something—like the guy who killed the therapist's wife, how his name was Marion Ette. You know, Marionette—like the puppets that people put strings on and stuff like that. My wife pointed that one out to me. And the title—oh my goodness, even the title was great! A Murder of Blackbirds—it just has such a nice ring to it! And how all the different lives of the different patients crossed each other and no one saw it coming! I mean, how do you even come up with that stuff? It was so good—all of it was so good! Well, except . . ."

"Except?" Russell asked intrigued.

"No, Mr. Prey, it is not my place to correct a great book-smart writer like yourself. I—I shouldn't have said anything."

"All right . . . well . . ."

"It's just," Mr. E interrupted, "it's just there was one bit you got wrong. One bit that all those murder stories get wrong."

"Oh? And which bit would that be?" Russell asked as he leaned back in his chair.

"The murdering part," the man with the yellow eye said in a hushed tone. "When I do read, I look for books about killers and murderers and, as great as you writers are and as much as you guys do get right about so much else, the actual murdering part you all get wrong. Maybe that's because words ain't been invented for how it feels to actually kill a man." He slowly beat the hammer into his leg, reflecting. "The rush of it all—like—like having sex for the first time. The foreplay of stalking the prey around, waiting for the perfect moment to indulge in the lust that's been building up inside you. Trying to savor every second, not wanting to rush things or move too fast. The pleasure of finding the perfect spot to fool around, a place warm and alone where you know you won't be rushed or interrupted." The hammer beat faster. "The ecstasy of the final moments of the chase, when you know what's coming and you can hardly wait for it anymore. Then the beauty and intimacy of the climax before one of you will go to sleep forever." The hammer stopped as the visitor leaned forward toward his host. "Mr. Prey . . ." the yellow eye called out.

"Ye—," Russell stammered as he cleared his throat. "Yes, Mr. E?"

"I . . . am . . . just . . . messing with you, brother!"

Mr. E straightened up before letting out a belly-shaking howl. "You—you should have seen your face!" Mr. E gasped for air between crooked cackles. "I can't—I can't believe I got you with that! You looked so scared!"

Not fully knowing what was happening, Russell began a nervous laugh of his own.

"I was just joshin' with you, Mr. Prey!" the man said, wiping away a tear from his cheek. "I thought it would be funny to try to get you with that—and by the looks of things, you've been got!"

Russell forced a laugh. "You did have me there for a second."

"I'm a bit of a kidder, and when I saw you in here writing, I thought to myself, I wonder if a little nobody like me could spook this

11

here big shot scary writer. So I figured I'd have a go at it! Between you and me, I just can't believe that I have done scared the Donn Angelos master of horror himself! My wife ain't gonna believe this!"

"You—you sure got me!" Russell groaned with relief. "Looks . . . looks like there is a new master of horror in town."

"Master of horror?" repeated Mr. E. "I like that. Say, I know this is out of the norm, but is there any way you could let me take a gander at what your new story is about? I just know my wife would be thrilled if—"

"No!" Russell exclaimed a little more forcefully than he'd intended. "No, no, sorry. It's . . . uh . . . it's just supposed to be top secret until it's published." The last thing Russell wanted was any possible chance of the discolored eye accidentally uncovering the recently omitted passage.

"Okay, okay. I get that. I really do. I get it," Mr. E said with a tinge of disappointment. "But, man!—what it must be like to be in your brain! To come up with all those nifty ideas. For once, I would just love to get in your head. I would love to be inside your mind and just watch you tick. To settle in your bones and look out through your eyes—to be Russell Prey for a day. My, what a perfect day that would be."

For a second time in their conversation, the peculiar peeper fixated on Russell.

Hoping this was another poor attempt at humor, Russell sat paralyzed in the tense silence.

"Well, I had better go get that window," said the repairman as he turned his head, the saffron sphere never shifting its gaze. "I'll be back before you can say, 'Watch out, it's Mr. E.'" With those parting words, Mr. E saw himself to the door and then left.

Russell sat quietly, long after the door had shut and the visitor had gone. On the one hand, he felt completely terrified in both what his recent acquaintance had said and the ominous tone with which he'd said it, but on the other hand he felt an unanticipated rush of creativity surging through his imagination. Every story needed its villain, and his had just exited the scene. Although he didn't fully know what the story would be about, he knew who his antagonist would be, and that was more than he needed for the time being.

Russell began to craft his narrative—one about a brilliant, ruggedly handsome author whose physical strength was outmatched only by his mental muscles—who was struggling to pen a second work to follow the massive success of his first book. Like all the main characters, the author's name would have the privilege of carrying on his own initials, R. P. This was, after all, one of the few trademarks of his storytelling, and a tradition he was proud to maintain.

Russell continued to weave his tale about a man who was a huge fan of the fictional author in his book. Over the years, the man had become obsessed with the author's undeniable exquisiteness, unbelievable talent, unforgettable wit, and unshakeable charm. Then the writer wrote about how, when a flying bird came crashing through the window, this psycho fan jumped at his chance to come face to face with his idol—perhaps even creating the situation by throwing the broken creature in himself. Then the crazed man dressed himself up in the costume of a repairman and arrived at the author's house mere minutes after a call had been placed to the repair shop.

Russell's fingertips were fountainheads showering the page. Everything was coming together so perfectly; the words were practically writing themselves. Through the open window, the sound of rain hitting the sidewalk resonated as unceasing applause. The bass from upper apartments played as an anthem of inspiration, while the shouting of angry tenants funneled in through the uncovered hole as wildly excited cheers.

Russell advanced the story to include a scene where an uncomfortable conversation between the two main characters led to the disguised villain—whose name he had not yet definitively decided, but probably began with an "E"—ominously telling the beloved author that he wanted to be inside him to experience his genius. Then, instead of fixing the window, the villainous visitor would place a special adhesive on the sides of the windowpane that would dry up in a matter of hours, thus allowing the window to pop right out of its socket in due time. At that point, after the window had been superficially repaired, the pseudorepairman would hide himself outside the author's house until it was dark and the wonderful wordsmith went to sleep. Then, in an unexpected blunder, the window would come crashing onto the living room floor, jolting the author awake. Not wanting to let the opportunity slip, the old buzzard would climb inside the house and into the author's room where he would proceed to take out the author's brain and wear his skin like the repairman costume he had donned earlier that day.

A little violent, Russell thought, *but the kids are so desensitized, they'll eat that stuff up!*

Ultimately, Prey concluded his novella with the madman putting on the author's clothes, placing the skinned body of the writer inside a large suitcase, and leaving the house on a journey to find a proper burial plot.

And just like that, he was done.

Never before had Russell finished a manuscript so fast. He was almost positive that halfway through typing, his fingers had caught fire and smoke had billowed out of his computer keyboard, but he never stopped to check, not when pure inspiration had a hold on him like a man possessed with poetic purpose.

Prey proceeded to review his work when he heard a sound coming from outside. It was starting to get a little dark out, the tangerine Donn Angelos sun just beginning to descend into a dream of summer. The rain had momentarily ceased its cadence, leaving a hue of humidity in its absence and making it all but impossible for him to see clearly into the night air.

Shrugging his shoulders, he returned to reading his masterpiece until he heard a different kind of clamor coming from the kitchen. He rose to inspect, but his body wouldn't move forward. Along with Russell, it waited for what would come next. His ears strained to absorb every sound as he anticipated his fiction coming to life.

As soon as he pinpointed the location of the noise, it would move.

At one time he could have sworn it was coming from the corner closet, but now it seemed to come from the creak of the ceiling fan that circled above him. It was the breeze coming through the window that rustled the pages of unused notes tacked to the bulletin board behind him. It was the movement of the unwashed plates in the kitchen sink as they nestled into their final place of rest. It was the ticking of the clock whose hands were clapping, tapping, rapping on its glass enclosure; the outdoor air conditioner that was breathing, wheezing, teething on the broken limbs of splintered sticks that had fallen from exposure.

And now the sound was coming from the bedroom.

The living room.

Across his desk.

Behind him.

Beside him.

Coming.

It was then that the front door flew open and Russell lunged backward in self-defense.

"Mr. Prey, are you okay?" asked Mr. E as he hurried in to help the startled writer.

"I'm fine," he declared as he brushed himself off. "I'm—what exactly did you see when you came in?"

"Nothing much—just you jumping back and landing on the ground is all. Everything okay, Mr. Prey?"

"Yes, yes. I'm fine—really." Russell couldn't help but smile as he laughed at himself for the way he reacted. "I guess I'm just a better writer than I thought. Thanks for the help."

Mr. E's eye beamed with happiness. "Happy to have been here to help. And you most definitely are a good writer! No doubt about that. No doubt at all. I suppose I'll go fix that window now." The grin slowly faded from his face, his blue eye blinking while the other held its steadfast stare.

"Say, Mr. E, can I ask you something?" asked Russell as the repairman turned to leave, unable to contain his curiosity any longer. "If you don't mind my asking—I couldn't help but notice that one of your eyes is—"

Mr. E turned around slowly. "Yellow? You want to know about my eye? Well I can't blame you for askin'. I'd ask too if I were you seeing this for the first time," Mr. E began, pointing to his golden gem while shuffling toward the speculative storyteller. "Not much to tell, really. You see, I come from what you might call a family of scavengers—good folk who work hard without much to show for it. Daddy worked as a repairman while my mama patched together a living working odd jobs to provide for me and my brothers and sisters. Six of us in all. Anyway, coming by a fresh meal wasn't always an option. The sad truth of the matter was that daddy pissed away most of the money he earned drinking the cheap whiskey he and his buddies made. Didn't give a damn about us. So Mama did the best she could to put food on the table, but some nights we were so hungry, and she didn't have any food in the house to give to us.

"Now, I don't see any baby pictures and don't see no toys thrown all over your carpet, so I don't think you got no kids, but as a man with a boy myself there just ain't no sound in the world like a hungry child crying. It makes somethin' in you just wanna do whatever you can to get them fed. And the type of good mama I had, well, my mama would rather starve herself than not have her chicks eat. So, on the nights when we couldn't afford to have any food in the house, she would send us out in pairs on down to the highway that ran not too far from our house, to scrounge up the meat of the animals laid out on the road—the ones hit and killed by the cars passing through."

Inwardly cringing, Russell nodded sympathetically as Mr. E continued. "All a bit unusual, I know. I know it's not the type of thing a 'proper person' would do, what a 'civil person' would do, but, like I done said, unless you've ever experienced what it is to be truly hungry—to be starving, you and your family, without any help in sight—you will never understand the depths a person will go to survive."

As Mr. E spoke, Russell watched the yellow eye swell in size as everything except it faded.

"Well, what Mama didn't know—what none of us knew then—

was that those animals sometimes carried diseases from the flies, maggots, worms, and other animals that had been chewing on their carcasses. Diseases that make your stomach turn sour, your skin break out in hives, your teeth rot, your gums bleed, and, in some extremely rare and serious cases, your eyes to discolor with infection. That's what happened to me, Mr. Prey. When Mama first saw what had happened to me, she damn near had a heart attack rushing me over to the doctor. At that time there was nothing they could do for me. A few years back, my wife bought me some of those contacts that change a person's eye color. She bought me blue ones on account of those being her favorite color for a man's eyes—blue. She always wanted to marry a man with blue eyes, and since she couldn't stand to see the real color of mine anymore, she bought me these colored contacts. I only got one in right now—lost the other earlier, when the wind blew something in my eye."

"That's a shame," Russell said. "I'm sure they're pricey."

"Yeah, and I don't like 'em. They try to change what mama nature gave me. They cover the truth and make me appear tame instead of the scavenger I really am."

With that, he put his hand on Mr. Prey's shoulder and began to laugh. "But don't worry—it's not contagious if that's what you're askin'!"

Unnerved, Russell exhaled a forced laugh, trying to ignore the diseased yellow stench that he perceived to be coming from the eye. Seeing that the story had been drawn to a close, Mr. E returned to the window, promptly placing the new glass into its frame and sealing off any small openings before stepping back to survey his work. "And that should do it," he said taking his gloves off and sticking them into his back pocket. "Good as new. Like nothing ever happened."

Russell was indescribably relieved. "Wow—great! That sure is great news. Thanks so much. It looks great." Anxious to be free of the putrid eye, which he was sure he could smell, Russell reached into his pocket and pulled out the largest single bill he could find. "Here—this is for all your hard work." It was more of a bribe to leave than a payment for services.

Mr. E took it in both hands. "Mr. Prey, you are way too generous. It has been simply life-changing getting to know you. I just can't wait to see the look on my wife's face when she hears that I was here working on your house!"

"It's been interesting to meet you as well," responded Russell, practically closing the door in the face of the repairman. "Have a good night now."

"I'll be seeing you soon! Best of luck on that new book of yours! I can't wait to read it!"

"Uh-huh. Thank you. Bye-bye now," said Russell as he closed the door and locked it soundly. As he walked back to his desk, the stench still lingered heavily in the air.

What is that smell? he thought as he plugged his nose. He strode into the kitchen in search of an air freshener, and there he realized the source of the rot. The foul odor emanated off the tiny dead bird lying softly on its bed of tissues. He picked up the bloodied tissues by their corners so as not to touch the baby vulture and headed to the back door, which he unlatched with his pinky fingers. He cracked the door open and flung the bird off the tissues as far as it could go. *Maybe the cat will find it and eat it*, he thought as he locked the door.

The day was ending fast, so Russell nibbled on some leftovers and headed up to bed. He was drained and had an early appointment set up with his sister, who frequently doubled as his editor, to review his manuscript in the morning.

Setting his alarm, he got under the covers and turned off the lamp that sat close by on his nightstand. The day had at last come to an end, the exhaustion of creativity pushing him to rest his mind much earlier than normal. He was proud of the day's achievement. His mind leisurely lingered over his new story as he eased into a light sleep.

Suddenly, a sound jolted him awake.

It was like something coming to life from the pages of his book. It was the sound of a window falling out of its frame.

It was the sound of fate with eyes of hellfire stepping on broken glass.

CHAPTER 2

CONTACT

For a woman who didn't believe in God, Alondra Pittas couldn't stop praying.

Tears filled her eyes and mascara ran down her light brown cheeks as she pleaded and bargained with any supernatural power willing to listen. "Oh God, let me find my son," she said. "Please, let me find my son. Please, God, let me find my son! Please, let him be all right. Just let him be all right."

For over eight hours, she'd scoured every inch of Donn Angelos' back roads, major highways, dirt paths, city streets, and residential crossings that were within a 30-mile radius of her house. She desperately looked for a sign—any visible evidence that her son was all right. He hadn't come home from school the day before, which was completely out of character for him. He knew they had plans. He knew that this year, his senior year, was extra special and that his mother wanted to take him out on a mother-son date to celebrate his accomplishment.

She'd been saving up for months to take him to the restaurant he had been talking about since freshman year—a high class, five-star kind of place where his favorite Orlando soccer players would congregate to sign autographs for fans and share stories of life on the field. With the salary she made, it was difficult to afford, but for months she'd been saving as much as possible from each paycheck. She'd even taken a second job in the neighboring town of Winter Haven, working the books for Floor Restore & More. And now, after months of sacrifice, she finally had just enough for the two of them to enjoy an unforgettable night together before he went off to college early, on a soccer scholarship. Practice was to begin in a week and that meant he would only stay in town for a few days before moving up to school to get settled in.

She was so proud of him for going to college. Every time she thought of him alone and away from Donn Angelos, she got a lump in her throat. But it wasn't that she didn't want him to go—it really wasn't. God knew she was proud of him for being the first in his family to get a college education since their family's emigration from Puerto Rico in the late 1950s. It was just that it had always been the two of them. Mother and son against the world, beating the odds. Every year on the last day of school, they met up and celebrated another level of completion, from the time he was seven to the time he was seventeen.

Nothing stood in the way of mother-son time. Nothing.

That's why Alondra knew something was wrong. If her son, her baby boy, had never missed a single celebratory dinner in all those years, why, at the time most special to her, most worth celebrating, would he disappear?

Something wasn't right. A mother knew when something isn't right. A mother knew.

Her suspicions were only verified when she found his car stranded in the school parking lot. When Alondra called her friends earlier that day and asked if they'd seen her son, they all laughed at her for worrying. "He's a teenager," they said. "He's probably off partying, enjoying the last day of class. That's what all teens do nowadays. Leave him alone—he'll be home when he's ready." Her son wasn't perfect;

Alondra knew that. She hadn't forgotten the night he'd come home drunk from that party after his soccer match. She hadn't forgotten how she'd had to kneel with him on the bathroom floor, warm washcloth in hand, holding his head like a newborn babe so that he didn't choke on his own vomit.

But that's exactly why she knew that wasn't the reason he was missing.

Her son was aware of the pain that his partying had inflicted on her, how disappointed she was in him for getting drunk. He had seen the triple shift she'd worked to make up the lost hours spent caring for him. When he looked her in the eyes and promised that he would never drink again, she knew he meant every word.

He couldn't be off at some party. Not my Jeremy, she thought, her hands stiff from clutching the steering wheel for so long. Something was wrong, terribly wrong. "God, please let me find my son. Please let him be okay. I promise I will go to church more— we both will go to church more. I promise I'll do anything you want. I just want my son back. Please just give me my son back." Her tears began once again to fall, tracing the salt patterns down her cheeks. The road was getting blurry now. Her contacts were dry and itchy after the night of searching for her darling boy. To make matters worse, the early morning fog had descended heavily on the desolate backwoods trail that looped and winded toward the marshy badlands of town. She could hardly make out anything in front of her.

She knew she had to pull over. She knew she had to just stop for a minute and rest her eyes. But she couldn't do it. She couldn't stop the search now. There had to be an alternative. Alondra rubbed her eyes, steering her old Chevy with her knees.

That's when the unthinkable happened.

The steering wheel became loose from between her knees as the car began to veer violently, throttling her off the road. She tried to correct the car, her tires feebly clinging onto the gravel. In a state of panic, Alondra overcorrected her vehicle into fast approaching traffic.

The last thing she heard as her Chevy crossed lanes was the sound of screeching and screaming. The force of the collision ricocheted her vehicle back several feet.

Alondra's head hit the steering wheel, and she lost a contact lens on impact. Her nose and lip were bleeding, and her legs were badly bruised. Her head throbbed as she tasted the metallic blood dripping into her mouth.

Dizzily, she tried to open her driver's side door, but her hand couldn't grasp the door handle. Looking down, it became clear that her arm was broken. Emotionally broken and physically battered, things began to go dark for Alondra as she slipped gently into the pardon of unconsciousness.

When she finally awoke, she knew she had to do something immediately about her arm, which was swelling and turning a greenish purple. She recalled constructing a makeshift sling for her son after he'd broken his arm during his freshman soccer season. Taking her belt off, Alondra looped the leather around her neck and set her fractured arm in place with the tenderness and patient precision of setting a broken bird's wing. Once her arm was secured, she opened the door and stepped clumsily out.

That's when she remembered that another car had been involved. The other vehicle, a grey compact car, had jolted off the side of the road and plowed nose first into the swamp where the algae-covered water met the decaying woods. The horn was stuck as it bellowed and gurgled in the murky waters as smoke filtered off the sides of the damaged hood.

"Oh, God, no! Please, God, not this," Alondra cried as she limped forward. "Hello? Hello, is everybody okay?"

Silence answered her.

As she neared the wreckage, she could see that thick, jagged tree limbs had impaled the windshield. It was then that she saw the blood pooling out of the driver's side of the car, swirling in the brown waters and dying the rims of the lily pads. With her shoes slightly hanging over the edge of the slope, she leaned forward, trying to balance while assessing the conditions of the vehicle's inhabitants. It appeared that both the driver and the passenger—a man and a woman from what she could make out —were dead.

Alondra tore her gaze away. The gruesome sight was too violent for her to handle. Even with her eyes closed, she couldn't get the picture out of her head. Stumbling a few steps back, she vomited, her stomach and mind both trying to purge the images she had seen. And then, with a force stronger than the accident itself, a terrifying thought struck her: *Was this my son?*

She dashed back to the edge, her good arm stabilizing her against the trunk of the sinking car. "Jeremy!" she cried. "Jeremy!" She had seen a car like this on several occasions in their neighborhood, parked near their house. What if one of Jeremy's friends let him drive their car after an all-nighter? What if in trying to save her son, she'd killed him?

She picked up a tree branch and stuck it through the shattered driver's side window. "God no, God no, no, no, no, please, please," she cried as she pressed the end of the stick against the back of the driver's head, tilting the left side of his jaw. With enough pressure she could see that the man's face had been completely beaten in. There was no way for her to tell for sure if this was her son.

She looked closer at the other details of his persona. The driver's clothes didn't match anything she'd ever seen him in, but he could have borrowed clothes from whoever he was partying with. The hair didn't seem like his either, but there was so much blood that she just couldn't tell.

"Oh God, oh God, please, please."

Had she been the one to kill her own son? In her frantic search to find him, praying to God for his safety, had she brought on him the fate that she most feared?

Then she saw it. A wedding ring.

Her son may have been a lot of things, but a married man was not one of them. Putting her hand over her mouth, she began to cry. "It's not him! Oh God, it's not my boy! Thank you, God! Thank you, God."

But a whimper came from the back seat. Shocked, Alondra craned her neck to see inside the contorted car.

It was a boy—seven years of age at the most—passed out in the backseat of the car, drenched in blood, tree sap, and slowly rising swamp water. He was clenching what appeared to be the shattered remains of a ceramic vase.

At this point the reality set in.

Alondra had killed two people. Through her selfish, negligent driving, she had caused the deaths of two innocent souls—the parents of this now orphaned child. And while she was rejoicing in the fact that her own son wasn't the one in the car, she had overlooked the humanity of the individuals who unfortunately were. Her hands were stained with their blood, their deaths on her conscience.

But she couldn't think about that. She still hadn't found her Jeremy.

The accident was terrible—and Alondra readily acknowledged that—but what about her son? Her mind raced. *Someone had to call the police, right? Someone had to take the blame for what happened in the accident, right?* she debated with herself as the car sloshed and settled a bit deeper in the waters.

Alondra turned around to assess the damage to her car. There was sizable damage to her side of the vehicle, but it appeared quite drivable. *They sure don't make them like they used to*, she thought.

With the car able to run, she could continue the search for Jeremy. Was her broken arm in pain? Absolutely, but it was nothing compared to the agony of her broken heart. There was no question about it: she had to find her son.

But what should she do about the accident? She couldn't just leave the scene of the crash! That would be morally wrong, wouldn't it? Alondra knew that she had an ethical responsibility to both herself and the victims of the accident. But what was the right thing to do?

The car accident had happened. It was terrible; it was horrible; but it was over. People were dead, but they weren't people that she knew or cared for. At the end of the day, they were just dead bodies. It was hard for Alondra to admit this, but it was the cold hard truth. They were strangers who were gone now, and there was nothing more that anyone could do for them.

But her Jeremy was still very much alive.

It was awful what had happened to those poor people, but was it right to let her son remain missing? Did two wrongs make a right? Enough people had been hurt in the car accident. Jeremy didn't need to be wounded by it too. He was a good boy, a loving boy, a boy who needed someone to find him and protect him.

A boy that needed, more than anything, his mother.

Besides, how sure was she that the accident was entirely her fault? She wasn't the only one who could have swerved out of the way. She wasn't the only one with the responsibility to drive safely on the road. After all, it hadn't been the severity of the accident that had killed those people, but the path the vehicle took afterwards—something that was completely out of her control and certainly something she shouldn't be held responsible for. The decision to swerve that particular way had been the driver's and the driver's alone. He made the choice, and he suffered the consequences.

Their deaths were not her fault. It was theirs, and there were no witnesses left alive to say otherwise. They would not be on her conscience. They would not be her problem.

She had to find her son.

It was then that her concentration was broken by the cries of the child in the backseat. "Mama," he whimpered. "Mama."

I can't just leave him out there, she resolved. The car could sink to the bottom of the swamp and he would drown, or a snake or alligator or some other slithering thing could swim into an opening and kill him, or if no one discovered him soon he may die of dehydration or starvation.

But how could she help both of the boys who needed her in that moment? There was no way she could save the child—not with her arm the way it was—and even if she were somehow able to rescue him, what then? Then he would know what she looked like. Then he would know who she was. Then, no matter how pressing her situation or what a good Samaritan she had been, he would send the police after her the first chance he got.

No, she couldn't save the boy herself; there was just too much risk in it.

But she was not the type of person to abandon a child trapped in the back of a sinking car. Leaving the crash scene was crime enough, but leaving a child to die? Limping over to her car, she felt for the cell phone in her pocket and dialed 911. She wouldn't stick around for the police and ambulance to arrive, and she certainly would never admit to being in any accident, but she would call and report the crash for the sake of the boy.

Then Alondra disconnected the call before it could go through. What if the police traced the call? They would have her number and place her at the scene of the accident.

She could go to jail for that. She couldn't risk going to jail, not with Jeremy still missing.

Getting back in her vehicle, she sat in the solitude of the unfrequented back road. Alondra cranked on the engine, which sputtered and gasped in disapproval before eventually allowing her to move forward. But it was no matter. Alondra had made her decision. She would do her part and pray to the God she hoped existed that someone would travel this way and save the child.

Deep down, Alondra knew that somewhere, somewhere closer than she could imagine, was another boy crying for his mama, waiting for her to come to his aid. That was the boy she needed to rescue.

She wasn't a criminal. *After all,* thought Alondra, *a criminal is a mother who doesn't take care of her son.*

CHAPTER 3

MOON PIES AT MIDNIGHT

H e dreamed about her again last night. This made it the sixth time this week. She had on her blue dress, the one she routinely wore with her white cardigan for their afternoon strolls through the park. It had always been his favorite dress, although he couldn't remember if he'd ever told her that. In his dream, she was in the kitchen baking his favorite dessert, pecan pie. It was the kitchen from their first home—the one with the stove that he often had to kick to turn on, the same one where the old lime green fridge sat humming in the corner. God, how he'd hated that fridge. He had forgotten about it until he saw it basking there in the dream.

She stood at the counter, her back turned as she swayed to the melodies of Frank Sinatra and the golden age of swing, humming lightly as she placed dishes in the soapy sink water. He had just come home from work, barely having enough time to loosen his tie, when the aroma of freshly baked crust, vanilla extract, and chopped pecans invited him to the kitchen.

He leaned against the wall, silently staring in wonder at the woman he had been blessed to marry. She looked so beautiful, curly blonde hair pulled back, green eyes gently focused on her task. He marveled at the casual grace that accompanied her every movement. She was the only woman he had ever known who was capable of making the most ordinary task worth marveling over. He walked over to her, wrapped his arms around her expectant stomach, and rested his head next to hers. His whole world was in that tiny broken kitchen—everyone he had ever or would ever love in his lifetime. It was his heaven, and she his angel. He could feel her smile as their bodies swooned in harmony to the music. "You're finally home," she said softly, reclining in her husband's strength.

"I am finally home," he replied.

And that's when he woke up.

He felt the oxygen cannula in his nose and the disposable bed liner beneath him. A rainbow of fluids, nozzles, gauges, and wires all crossed and intertwined over the backdrop of his beige room, spiraled in spectral spectacle as he unwillingly witnessed the marvels of modern medicine. He should have passed when she did. His body should have been allowed to die as his heart had that day, but here he was, bound to an involuntarily prolonged life. He spent his days inhaling the relentless stench of stale bleach and lukewarm antiseptics used in the nursing home, as a constant barrage of squeaking white tennis shoes, irritated heart monitors, and hissing oxygen tanks reminded him just how far he was from home.

He tried closing his eyes, but the dream was as distant as the lifetime it represented. He now lay still, cold sweat collecting on his forehead and matting down his snowy hair. He watched through his second-story window as the dark sky cried, its tears slowly running down the glass pane. "Good morning, Sarah," he said to himself. "I hope to come home to you today, my darling." And as that prayer passed his lips, a familiar face entered the room.

"Good morning, Mr. Dearly. How are we doing today?" A plump young African American attendee smiled, holding a silver clipboard in her hands, her pink polka-dotted scrubs clinging to her in odd places.

"I'm doing better than I deserve," he responded, trying to force a smile. "What do you have for me today, Tonya?"

"Well, Mr. Dearly, today—"

"For the last time, Tonya, call me Ernie. Mr. Dearly makes me sound old," he interrupted, a real smile finding its way to the surface.

"Okay, Ernie." She chuckled. "It's good to see you've got a little more of your fire in you today. Lord knows we've been needing it 'round here! Here's some breakfast for you—and your pills." She lifted a soufflé cup full of candy-coated medicines, each one bulkier than the last.

He took his pills and chased them down with a small cup of orange juice. Then came his favorite part of the day—the daily *Bonanza* marathon followed by back-to-back episodes of *Matlock*. Once these episodes were over, it was time for lunch. Right on cue, Tonya brought him the special of the day: sliced turkey, mixed vegetables, and a cup of chocolate pudding, which he immediately sent back with her in exchange for two Moon Pies.

After lunch, per his daily routine, he opened one of the Moon Pies, taking a moment to breathe in its unique chocolatey scent, and proceeded to eat it with slow, exacting precision. The second Moon Pie, however, he left untouched.

From noon to three there was a mini marathon of *In the Heat of the Night*, after which came miscellaneous Westerns that Ernie enjoyed the most. He often caught himself asking, "What did you think of that one, Sarah?" to the empty chair beside him. He used to watch all of his Westerns with her. It wasn't that they were his favorite shows, but on days like today, with the television up and a Western program on, it was as if she were sitting right beside him in her old little rocking chair, knitting something small to send off to one of their grandchildren. It wasn't quite the home he was used to, but anywhere he felt her presence was home enough.

In the evening, Tonya brought his supper. It was the Friday special: leftover turkey slices with mashed potatoes and two Moon Pies on the side.

"Tonya, my dear, you are too good to me," said Ernie as he began to unwrap the plastic Moon Pie wrapper, his hand tremors getting the best of him. She smiled and opened the package for him.

As Ernie took a big bite of his much-appreciated treat, Tonya said, "Mr. Dearly, can I ask you a question?"

"Is the question, 'Can I call you Ernie?' Because, if so, the answer is yes."

Tonya smiled and continued. "Now I've been your caretaker for, what would you say? About seven months?"

Ernie paused and did a little mental math. "Seven or eight . . . something like that."

"Now, Mr. Ernie, every meal for these past seven or eight months, I've seen you eat your meal and then ask for Moon Pies. Over and over I've seen you do it. And because you're such a nice man, I always make sure to get them for you. From the look of things in the kitchen, we might not be getting anymore for some time. So, with that said, I was wondering—"

"Wondering if there was something else I would like instead?" Ernie asked as he took another bite.

"I can get you a lot of things—the kitchen staff have more pudding and Jell-O cups than they know what to do with. Is there anything else I could get for you?"

"Is it the expense? Because I have some money I can give you to pick them up for me." Ernie shifted in his bed and reached for his sock drawer where he had stashed some cash.

"Maybe you could eat those second Moon Pies after you get done eating the first? I've never seen you eat the second. And maybe that way you could have some rationed out until we figure what to do?"

"I appreciate the suggestion, but I can't do that," Mr. Dearly solemnly replied. "I'm saving them for someone else."

"For someone else?"

Ernie nodded and popped the last bite into his mouth.

"Well, maybe they can start pitching in to get you some more. In the meantime, I'll try to figure something out." With a wink, she collected his plate, making sure to leave the uneaten Moon Pie behind.

As the sun set, Ernie embraced the reality that one more day had drawn itself to a close. One more day with no letters, phone calls, or visitors. One more day without a reason for one more day.

Returning his bed once again to its prostrated position, Ernie closed his eyes as the late night reruns sang him a final lullaby and he drifted off to sleep.

And there, in the depths of unconsciousness, he heard it.

"Ernest, Ernest," he heard a warm voice begin to say. "Ernest, it's time to get up now. Ernest, my darling, it's time to get up."

Mr. Dearly smiled. He could recognize that voice anywhere.

"Sarah," he said. "I've been waiting for you."

He opened his eyes and saw his wife sitting in the empty chair next to his bedside, her left hand grabbing his as she ran her right hand through his feathered hair. She was wearing her blue dress with the white sweater that he liked so much, her silvery hair pulled back into a bun. She looked exactly as she did the last time he saw her—like an angel. "Ernest, it's time to come home," she said as she helped him up out of bed.

"No, sweetheart, my chair. I need my wheelchair," he responded, stopping her before she positioned him too far off the bed.

"Not today, Ernest. Try to walk and you'll see."

He mused at her unsupported confidence in his walking ability. Ernest knew that he wouldn't be able to walk—he hadn't been able to take a single unassisted step off his cot in over a year. But, never wanting to displease his darling, he hung his withered legs over the side of the bed and slowly placed them on the floor. Then, inching little by little with the help of his wife, he leaned forward enough to stand up.

"Here goes nothing," he said to himself as he put all his strength into his rickety legs, fully expecting to need his love to catch him when he fell.

But he didn't fall. He looked down at his legs and then back up to Sarah in amazement. He put his hands out, resting some of his weight on her shoulders before he took his first step forward. With each step, Ernie gained confidence in the next until he no longer needed assistance to move on his own.

"I've laid out some clothes for you, Ernest," Mrs. Dearly said, interrupting his progress. "Why don't you get dressed into something a little more comfy?"

In all the excitement, Ernie forgot that he was wearing a hospital gown. "I wondered where the draft was coming from," he replied with a mixture of wonderment and excitement as he entered the bathroom to change. She had set out his favorite outfit—his short-sleeve, white button-up polo with his long grey pants, brown dress shoes, blue bucket cap, and tan rain slicker. He had never been more eager to get dressed in his life, thinking with every article of clothing how good it felt to be going home.

"Did you catch that Western I was watching?" he asked as he looked in the mirror, splashing English Leather cologne on his wrists and neck.

"I did, darling. It was a very nice episode."

"Well," he said tucking in any loose corners of his pressed polo, "what do you think?"

"You look very handsome, Ernest. A sight for these sore eyes."

"Shall we?" He offered his arm and a smile to his lovely bride. She giggled as she wrapped her arm in his, the rapture of first love renewed.

They meandered down the stairs, across the hall, and out the door, the whole walk feeling like a promenade through the clouds. By the time the two had departed, the rain had stopped, allowing the stars to be seen more clearly than either lovebird could recall. Ernie closed his eyes and filled his lungs with the crisp night air, a luxury he had foregone for far too long.

"It's such a nice night for a stroll, Ernest. Why don't we go on a walk about town—the kind of walk we used to take on nights like this?"

Ernie knew he couldn't refuse; the way her eyes sparkled up at him in the moonlight was all the convincing he needed. He pushed open the iron gates at the entrance of the nursing home, and they began their walk through the winding empty road.

Every Donn Angelos Main Street storefront they passed, every unoccupied lot and vacant building they strolled by reached out and offered a multitude of misplaced memories for Mr. Dearly. This was, after all, the town he had grown up in, the town he had grown old in. In each window, he saw the ghosts of time, reflections of days carelessly spent basking in the waning sun of youth.

As they passed the old meat market, Ernie saw himself as a child, skipping rope out on the sidewalk. His black hair covered by his favorite blue jean cap, his hand-me-down pants falling down and tripping him up at every jump because of their oversized length. Next to him were his two best friends Ryan Gaffney and Kyle Johnson, as they sat on the steps of the store reading the funny papers and chewing pink bubblegum. He had forgotten how many summers the three of them had shared, prying into mischief by day and sleeping under the stars at night. He wondered, as he watched, if either of his two best friends had sucked the marrow out of life as they all had vowed those many years ago; if they had ever actualized any of the grand schemes they concocted during those tender moments of adolescence before the world had begun molding them into its image. He wondered if they had ever found love, reconciled with God, or had families. His heart warmed at the prospect of the lives he hoped they lived.

Across the street from the meat market was Dixie's Diner, where Ernie had consumed much of his time and money on first dates. He remembered the 12-record jukebox that sat in the corner where he and his pals would listen to the latest tunes coming off the billboard charts, trying to entice girls over for a dance or two. Most fondly of all, Ernie remembered the last first date he ever took to Dixie's. A blonde-haired, green-eyed goddess who by grace alone went out for a milkshake with him one afternoon after school, in the fall of 1962. Her name meant princess and she lived up to the part. It was her hand that he was holding now as they took their stroll down memory lane.

But for every joyful recollection Ernie experienced, there were two that brought him before the threshold of remorse. Opportunities not taken, words not spoken, acts of kindness that he allowed to pass him by. He saw the moments of humiliation he had suppressed—when he missed the game-winning catch at his high school baseball tournament, when he'd been cornered by bullies after school, when he'd lacked the courage in college to stand up for his beliefs. He relived the dark hours of depression he experienced when he passed the doctor's office and beheld the memories of their first miscarriage, and when he passed the paint store where he had gone to get supplies to paint over their pink nursery during the fallout of their heartache. For each one of the memories he had of his wife and their two eventual miracle babies, he had two where something more pressing had stolen their time together, and in that sense the recollections he didn't have stung more than the ones he did. With each stop along the way, Mr. Dearly endured all the regret, shame, guilt, and sorrow that he felt in those initial times of agony and frustration. Unable to bear the brunt of this burden any longer, he slowly let go of his wife's hand and began to weep.

"Ernest, what's wrong?" Sarah asked, rubbing his back in an effort to soothe her aching husband.

"I . . . I just . . . I've lived all my life thinking that I was a good man—an honorable man. But in every store window we pass, I've seen clearly the reflections of the man I really am."

"Ernest," Mrs. Dearly responded, "my darling, if any could be called good or honorable, it would be you. But if you do not like the memories you see in their reflections, why don't you change what you see?"

"What do you mean?"

"Come here. I'll show you." Walking to the next window, she motioned for him to peer in. "Tell me what you see in here."

"I see our daughter, Linda. She looks about 12 years old, and she's sitting by herself at a table in the corner of the room. It appears to be some sort of dance. There is soft music playing and the lights are dimmed. There's a banner in the corner. It says Daddy-Daughter Dance." He stepped back from the sight and looked to his wife for clarification.

"You were supposed to go with her that night, darling, remember? She asked you weeks in advance, and you told her you would go. I sewed the green dress you see her wearing. She was so excited the night before, that she could hardly sleep. But the next day you stayed late at work and had to cancel on her. She was devastated. I told her to spend some time with her friends at the dance and to try to enjoy herself, and that I would pick her up soon. She sat there all night alone until I came and got her."

"Well, I'm sure I had a good reason for staying late at work. We were falling on rough times, and I was looking for a promotion, if I remember correctly. I'm sure that my not being there, as hurtful as it was for Linda, was for the betterment of our family. I never did anything without double-checking that I was putting our family first," Ernie responded, defaulting into his old automatic defensive rationalization.

"Yes, my dear, you were able with that money to help us pay some bills. But in the scheme of a lifetime, which is more important? To do things for your family, or to do things with your family? No amount of money can ever buy back that experience for our only daughter or purchase back that time you could have spent with her."

Ernie put his face back up to the window and looked in on his little daughter. "She was so sweet back then."

"She still is, Ernest. Why don't you go to her?" she asked.

"What do you mean?"

"These are not simply the shadows of things long passed, but events that are transpiring before your eyes in real time that you are able to stop and change. If you don't like the father you were, alter what you did. Step into any memory that you wish to change, and change it. Redeem yourself by being the man you have always wanted to be instead of the man you remember yourself as being."

Mr. Dearly paused, pondering the opportunity that life had just presented him. Could he really go back and right the wrongs of his past?

If there were such a place, it would be nothing short of heaven.

"What will you do, Ernest?" his wife asked. "Which man do you choose to be?"

With that, Mr. Dearly tucked in his shirt, took off his cap, combed his hair with his fingers, and gave his wife a kiss. Then he entered his own memory.

The room smelled like musk and cheese. A lonely disco ball spun in a corner as '80s records played over the loud speakers above. He looked around the room at all the other fathers dancing with their daughters. They all were wearing nice suede suits, their hair combed perfectly in place as they stooped down to dance with their children. He was twice their age, wearing his Tuesday best. *I shouldn't be here*, he thought. *I should just leave now. This is no place for a guy like me.*

But that's when he saw her. His little angel wearing the green dress her mother had made. White shoes coming up to her shins, a flower belt around her waist. She was too beautiful to be sitting all alone. He took a deep breath and walked forward.

"Hello, darling," he said. "May I have this dance?"

Linda looked up. "Daddy!" She smiled and ran to him, tackling him with a huge hug. He stroked her blonde hair as she held onto him, tears welling in his eyes.

"Yes, baby, daddy's here. Everything is all right."

From that point on, the couple were inseparable. They danced some and ate some, but mostly they talked. He asked her all sorts of questions—everything he had ever wondered about her but had never asked. He asked what she wanted to do in life, who her biggest crush was, how school was going, what classes she liked the most, what problems she was having. She gushed out information like a flowing faucet that had long been stopped up, looking the whole time as though she had never been so pursued by her father.

Ernie was on top of the world. At the end of the dance, all the fathers who came were honored with sashes that their daughters had made. His was pink with glitter, flowers, and the words *World's Best Daddy*. He beamed with pride as his little girl put her ribbon around his neck.

They left the dance, her tiny hand nestled in his, but as soon as they walked out the door, the memory was over and Linda was gone.

"Well, my darling," Sarah asked, "how was your evening?"

"It was incredible! Amazing! Our daughter is so wonderful to be around—so full of life and beauty. And she gave me this sash." He grabbed at his chest and pulled out his prize ribbon.

"That sounds wonderful, dear," she replied. "Is there anywhere else you would you like to go?"

Ernest led his wife from memory to memory as he raced to reclaim all the opportunities he had squandered during his life, collecting keepsakes along the way. He took his son to the baseball game he'd always meant to take him to and brought back their ticket stubs and a bright blue banner for the Donn Angelos Devils. He humbled himself to visit his father one last time, despite their ongoing feud, and received for his efforts the golden cross necklace he'd always admired. He made time to play with his granddaughter one last time, and she gave him a bracelet she'd strung together that said, "I Love Papa." Under the twilight of the heavens, Ernest Dearly became the man he had always hoped to be.

After walking through what remained of memory lane, Mrs. Dearly spotted a resting place on a bench in the park that the two liked so much, and led Ernest down for a sit. He put his prizes on the bench next to him as he sat down to take in the night air with the love of his life. He put his arm around her as she rested her head on his shoulder, the bell tower at the center of town lightly tolling 12 successive strokes in the distance.

"Ernest, have you had a nice day?" Sarah gently asked her husband.

"The best, my darling; the absolute best."

"And you've said all the things you wished to say, and done all the things you wished you'd done?"

"All that I can remember, my love," he answered, the sound of contentment resonating in his voice as he watched a meteor flicker across the night sky.

"And this place, Ernest—do you recognize this place?"

Noticing the peculiar tone in her voice, Ernie looked around to see what his wife was referring to. There were trees all around them and a lake that mirrored the moon like glass to their right. There was a concrete path that lay before them, the end of which rested an old dilapidated snack-shack where weary walkers welcomed scrumptious solace for their souls.

And that's when he recognized the spot in which they were sitting.

"Oh Sarah," he whispered, placing his hand over his mouth. He stood up and walked toward the small shack. "This is where . . ." He turned and looked at his wife, his hands shaking and his knees buckling beneath him. "I'm so sorry—I had no idea this was . . . I'm so sorry." He began to weep.

"It's all right, Ernest, everything is all right, darling. Tell me what happened here," Mrs. Dearly said, coaxing her husband on.

"We were here." His voice trembled as he put the event in order in his mind. "You were sitting right there where you are now. We were taking our afternoon walk in the park. And you were tired; you hadn't been feeling well all day. I told you to stay here. I told you to sit here and that I'd go get you something to eat."

"Yes, Ernest, go on."

"And that's when . . . oh God." Ernie had to stop. The memory was too painful for him. Tears streamed down his cheeks.

"It's all right, my darling. Keep going."

"That's when I left you to get you something to eat. I thought I was helping you by getting something to settle your upset stomach. You told me to stay with you—you begged me to stay. I told you that I would be right back. I wanted to surprise you by getting your favorite treat—I went to get you two of the Moon Pies that you liked so much.

I waited in line and turned around and that's when—that's when I saw you. You were slumped over on this bench. I tried to wake you but you wouldn't wake up. I called the ambulance, but they said it was too late. You were gone—you were gone and it was all my fault!"

"No, Ernest, it was not your fault, darling. It was a heart attack. It was no one's fault."

"I should have stayed with you. I should have stayed! I didn't even get to say goodbye."

"Then change that, Ernest," Sarah said as she stood and came to the aid of her sobbing husband. "You have a chance to change that now." Ernie looked up at her as she wiped away the tears from his eyes. "Stay with me, Ernest. Stay with me this time."

"Do you . . . do you still want me to?"

She smiled and, looking down, reached for his left hand that still bore his wedding ring. "Always and forever. Remember, darling? Our love is eternal; our love is enduring." She held his hand in hers as she kissed his eyelids. "Will you stay with me, my love?"

"Always and forever," he replied.

Hand in hand, the two lovebirds made their way over to their beloved bench. He placed his arm over her once again, and she rested her head in the strength of his shoulders as they waited to watch their first sunrise together in six years. It was the dawn of a new lifetime together; it was the beginning of eternal bliss.

The following morning, Tonya walked into Mr. Dearly's room to do her usual inspection, upon which she found a very unusual sight. Mr. Dearly was missing—gone from his bed and out of the nursing home. But in his place she found an assortment of memorabilia: a bright blue banner, tickets from an old baseball game, a gold necklace, a bracelet, a sash, two wedding rings, and two empty Moon Pie wrappers.

CHAPTER 4

THE HARBINGER

*L*ukas Eary might only have been in second grade, but his
eyes had seen a dragon—
*a beastly thing with tooth and wing who was best to be
left unchallenged,*
*a fiery yellow harbinger of death who knew no pity and sought
no rest,*
*a chrome-fanged titan who roamed to destroy, to put in its steel
belly any little boy*
*whose mother did not pick him up from school because he
misbehaved or broke the rules—*
*because he chewed bubblegum and ran through the halls, because
he feared not the brutish beast when it called.*
*So as recompense for past wrongs completed, these misbehaving
children were obliged to step up, step in, and be eaten.*
*Among those miserable mortals cast into the depths of this dragon
named school bus were Timmy Grime, Johnny Slime,*
and, of course, our hero Lukas.
*The breathtaking Princess Josephine was trapped in the brute as
she cried out . . .*

"Whatcha doin', Pukey Lukey?"

Lukas looked up from his journal to see fat Timmy looming over the blue bus seat in front of him, his camouflage hat on backwards revealing his Irish hair slicked back underneath.

"Ha-ha—Pukey Lukey! Good one, Tim," another fifth grader chimed in.

"What do you want, Timmy?" Lukas turned his eyes back to his work, pushing back the oversized glasses his parents made him wear.

"Oh nothin'. I'm just wonderin'," Timmy's sausage fingers quickly snatched the journal from Lukas's lap, "what you're writing in your little girly diary!"

"Hey! Give me that!" Lukas demanded, swatting and pawing for the notebook. At this point, Timmy's belly and flabby arms began jiggling profusely with laughter, his eyes squinting in pure delight.

"Let's read it and see what little Pukey Lukey has been writing all day!" The other kids egged him on.

Lukas tried to stand up and grab his journal back, but two of Timmy's friends—who were twice as big and twice as ugly—came and smushed him between themselves, holding him down.

"Mama couldn't pick me up from school again today, so I had to go to St. Jude and wait with the other kids," Timmy read with a mocking whine as his cronies cackled and feigned boohoos. "Father Michael and I talked a lot about summer plans and went over confirmation questions, and we played checkers while everybody but me and some other kids got picked up. They called Mama over and over, but they said she never picked up. The church told us at 6:00 that we all had to ride the bus. I hate riding the old school bus that the church drives us in. The bus driver is always angry, and it looks like a big, smelly, yellow dragon." Timmy snickered. "A dragon? There's no such thing as dragons! What a retard!"

"Yeah—a real retard! Ha-ha! Nice one, Tim!" one of Timmy's sidekicks yelled from the back of the bus.

"What else did the retard say?" another one jeered on in encouragement.

Timmy scanned through the lines looking for something juicy. "Nah—it's all stupid," his eyes enlarged, "except for this: Josephine has to ride the bus today too. All the other kids are mean except for her. I think she is so pretty. I wonder if she likes me?" The fifth grade fiend snarled with laughter, "Did you guys hear this? Pukey Lukey likes Josephine!" He pointed at the little blonde girl in the lime green sundress, sitting by herself in seat number 62—the seat directly across from Lukas. "Pukey Lukey and Grossy Josie! Pukey Lukey and Grossy Josie!" Timmy chanted, the whole school bus joining in.

Lukas winced in Josephine's direction, his expression apologizing for dragging her into the middle of everything.

"I don't like him! I don't like him! I don't like him!" she yelled out in self-defense. Lukas let his face fall toward the ground. His life had officially been ruined.

"You kids shut up back there!" the bus driver called out from the front, his eyes scanning the reflections of the children in his oversized rearview mirror. "You leave that boy alone! Now everyone sit down and shut up!" he commanded—and when Mr. Charon spoke everyone always listened. Rumor was that he used to take the naughty kids back to his house and eat them whole.

Timmy threw the journal back at Lukas and resumed his seat. It didn't matter, though. The damage had been done. Lukas was no longer in the writing mood. He propped his head on the window, his black hair leaving oil smudges where it lay. The sky was getting darker by the minute as the sun set into the storm clouds swelling over Donn Angelos.

Lukas looked down at his Velcro watch and impatiently bobbed his leg up and down. The bus ride always felt long, having no one to talk to, and now after being humiliated in front of Josephine, he just wanted to go home and hide. Looking at the kids left in their seats, Lukas estimated that they were about halfway to his house embedded within the Bomull Munn swamp, which was always the last stop.

He watched the overcast scenery outside as it was illuminated by the flashing lights on the sides of the repurposed bus. It was like seeing images through the lens of a slow motion strobe light. Snapshots of trees, cows, barbed wire fences, and trailer parks filled his vision. There was never much to see out of the window, here in the middle of no man's land. House . . . house . . . tree . . . fence . . . tree. He made a game of what he could see as the world blurred by. House . . . house . . . barn . . . cow . . . tree . . . tree . . . tree . . . tree . . . tree. They were now passing through the woodland marsh that spanned several miles before his home. This was the same marsh where his father used to take him fishing when he was younger, but they hadn't fished in a while, not since their financial situation had improved.

The rain was now falling so hard that it was nearly impossible to see anything outside. *Well, there goes that game,* he thought in disappointment.

But that's when he saw it. In the flash of the light he made out a figure standing in the rain up the dirt road.

The glimpsed image was so distorted that he thought he'd imagined it. Before he could determine what he had truly seen, the light ceased and the image disappeared into the blackness of the storm.

Lukas waited for the light to flash again.

When it finally did, the figure was standing at his window. A man in blue—maybe a jacket, a poncho, or trench coat—carrying something. A long something. Maybe a tree branch that fell in the storm, or a big bag of trash he was leaving out in the marsh, or luggage that he was taking with him back to his lair.

Once more, the light faded and the man vanished.

At this point, Lukas pressed his face up against the glass, his body teetering on the edge of his seat.

When the light flashed again, the man appeared in the rightmost edge of view from his window. Lukas strained to make out the man's face.

And what about the object? What was the man carrying?

Lukas's mind finally caught up with the image: it was a body.

The man was dragging a body—

That's what it had to be; nothing else was that size and shape.

The light passed once more, and Lukas looked around him to see if anyone else had seen what he had seen.

Unfortunately they were all on their phones—including the bus driver. Their faces glowed with indistinct colors, residue of cheap entertainment. Lukas spun back to his window in hopes that the man would appear again.

But he didn't.

When the light finally did reappear, there was only the marsh. Lukas opened his journal and began to write. He began constructing a story around the disconnected images he had seen:

> *A ghoul painted blue had done something cruel within the home of someone else.*
>
> *It was a creature half-human with both blood and venom surging through its pulse.*
>
> *Its sickly snake eyes were starving for murder, its appetite hungry to kill. So it slithered inside and paused to surprise whomever was appointed for hell.*
>
> *At that very moment, the blue-coated serpent saw a man enter the abode.*
>
> *He was carrying groceries, a book bag, and rosary, presuming no one was home.*
>
> *All alone, the man ate his meal, the beast allowing the mortal to eat, because the devil knew that the fool eating food would be fat and fresh for the feast.*
>
> *It was then, when the man's back was turned, that the snake made his move, slowly slithering from behind.*
>
> *In a flash of brilliance, he bit, sinking his teeth into it, swallowing the man whole in his prime.*
>
> *And leaving his face for dessert, the serpent began to exert itself toward its home in the dark, to its hole underground where it has never been found—the macabre and malevolent marsh.*

Just then, the old school bus screeched to a halt.

"Last stop," Mr. Charon said, his voice reverberating throughout the metallic hull.

Getting off the bus, Lukas stood on the edge of his long, crooked, downward sloping driveway and watched helplessly as the bus meandered off into night, his oversized backpack casting an eerie shadow. Looking through the rain to his house, he noticed that neither of his parents' cars were parked outside. *Guess I'm all alone tonight*, he thought, silently counting the number of times that week that his mother stayed late at work and his father ran late errands.

Mustering up his courage, Lukas began shuffling toward the front door, his shoes squishing each step along the muddy trail. Noises of the marsh were all around him, surrounding him, vying for his attention. Owls hooted in the distance; leaves rustled and wrestled one another. They were all sounds he'd heard a thousand times before.

But tonight, the typically friendly noises didn't comfort him. The leaves playing sounded more like the crunch of someone's shoes shuffling toward him, the owl's screech more a warning than a welcome. To his left he heard something large stepping in his direction; to his right something slithered and let out a yelp in the darkness. Everywhere he turned, Lukas could see ferocious eyes gleaming through the trees.

And perhaps among these eyes, a pair belonging to the man in blue. *It's okay*, he thought. *It's only my imagination. Any minute now, the house light will come on. The light sensors always come on. Any minute now.*

But the light never came on.

Lifting his arm into the rain, he tried to cause enough commotion to trip the light, but to no avail. Lukas suddenly became keenly aware of how far his closest neighbor was, a fact that had never before crossed his mind. It was just him and the creatures of the shadows for miles.

And they were all watching him.

The closer he splashed toward his house at the edge of the swamp, the higher the standing water around him rose. Broken beer bottles swirled between his legs, entangling them with Spanish moss and muck. Between the humidity and the musty rain, his glasses hindered more than helped, creating monstrous distortions wherever he looked.

Taking off his glasses to wipe them dry, he glanced down and saw that the water around him was teeming with earthworms displaced by the flooding swamp. Their slimy wriggling bodies in the moonlight together with the banshee cry of the overhead owls made for a scene of pure horror to the boy, as if the bowels of Hades had been opened with a thousand flesh-stripped writhing hands curling and clawing over one another as they reached up toward him, climbing onto him with their disjointed sticky fingers. Reaching down to push the worms off, he saw the long tail of something ahead of him dip underneath the dirty water as a splashing chomp to his right made him almost lose his footing.

Lukas reached into his pocket and pulled out the rosary that Father Michael had given him in preparation of his impending confirmation. "In the name of the Father, and the Son, and the Holy Spirit," he said as he crossed himself, holding his rosary close to his heaving chest. If he could just get inside, he would be safe. He just had to get inside.

"Hail Mary, full of grace."

Lukas quickened his pace as he made his way up to the house, his hair on end.

"The Lord is with thee."

What if the man in blue was lurking in the shade of the broken-limbed trees waiting to pounce? What if a hand raised out of the black waters and dragged him under?

Lukas could feel the eyes coming out of their shadows now, splashing into the water behind him; scores of scrawny severed fingers rippled onto his bare calves.

"Blessed art thou among women, and blessed is the fruit of thy womb, Jesus."

His prayer was getting faster now. His tongue and feet quickened with every step. He could feel something coming. He could feel the darkness reaching for him.

"Holy Mary, Mother of—"

Just then, a raccoon scurried past him, hissing as it went. Lukas practically jumped out of his skin. Lightning cracked behind him as he began to run toward the porch steps, his legs stifled by the living molasses water. There was a sloshing behind him now, the sound of something coming closer and closer. Something big; something possibly human.

"Pray for us sinners now!" he prayed louder.

The creature was almost on him now. Reaching the front step to the house, Lukas felt something grab his leg. A boney hand from the floodwaters was holding him, pulling him into the deep. Lukas lifted and pulled and shrieked until he unearthed a skeletal root that had gripped his shoe between the laces. Bolting up the other three stairs, he was now at the door, his back exposed to whatever it was that was still wading ever closer. His house keys trembled in his grasp as he felt worms crawling inside his clothing. The splashing behind him grew louder.

"And at the—"

The first step creaked behind him.

He couldn't unlock the door fast enough. He had the right key now—he was sure of it—but the key wouldn't work. He couldn't focus. It was hard to breathe.

He couldn't look back.

He had to get inside.

The second stair creaked under the weight of the thing behind him.

The snake coated blue was surely behind him.

The man beast was upon him, its breath curling on the edge of his ear. He could feel it reaching for his backpack.

He could feel the tickle of its tongue on the back of his neck.

"And—and at the hour of death!" he shouted, successfully twisting the key and opening the door to his house, scarcely alluding the fangs that were about to snap and drag him into the deep. He slammed the door behind him.

"Amen," he said as he propped himself up on the door. He was safe at last.

Safe and—alone.

Lukas then remembered that no one was home. He flipped on the light in the doorway, the lamps in the living room, kitchen, and den. He turned on every bulb that he could think of—inside and outside—in an attempt to flood the house with light.

Feeling fortified, he looked at the clock.

It was dinner time, but Lukas didn't feel like eating. His stomach was still in knots and his jilted nerves had transitioned into nausea. Leaving a muddy trail zigzagging through the house, Lukas kicked off his shoes and cleaned his glasses.

He entered his bedroom and quickly locked the door behind him. He removed his bulky backpack and sat on the edge of his bed, feeling not quite ready to expose his body to the elements of unconsciousness.

In an attempt to distract himself, Lukas got undressed and put on his superhero patterned pajamas to keep him safe. For some inexplicable reason they always reassured him that everything would be fine.

Walking over to his desk in the corner of his room, Lukas sat down to his ongoing game of Zibbyth: The Strange and Treacherous Journey—a role-playing game his mother had purchased for him as a belated birthday present. Lukas had heard how fun the game was to play with a group but, never having anyone to play with, he kept his own turn continuing as his character marched through the eight boards on his quest to defeat the evils of a mad scientist and his robot army.

Finally able to calm himself down, Lukas lay in bed, the lights continuing to glow protectively over him. He hadn't heard either of his parents' cars pull up yet, which was unusual for this time of night but, weighing the options, he decided to stay in his room rather than chance it by entering the hallway of the unknown to gain certainty, and possibly lose his life.

He pulled his blanket up over his body, covering it from head to toe, in case the snake-man paid him a visit. The boy knew that when his head was covered nothing could see him that he didn't want to.

Of course he knew it—it was science. He could finally sleep in peace knowing that he was invisible underneath his sheets. And besides, what were the chances of the snake-man finding him at home? Slim to none! With that reassurance, Lukas drifted off to sleep.

When the boy awoke, it was to the comforting sound of his mother's voice carrying through the house.

Mama's home! Everything will be all right now, he thought.

Lukas jumped out of bed and raced to his mama's voice, the sound of safety and shelter. She was in the den—only a few feet away. Running into the room, he cried out to her, "Mama! Mama!" His arms extended out, reaching for a much-needed hug.

But as he ran, he neglected to look down where he was stepping. Lukas's bare feet slipped on the muddy trail he had left earlier and he fell forward, crashing his head into the bookshelf above.

He was dizzy. His head throbbed and he felt blood ooze from the gash.

He began to cry as he lifted his arms out to his mother.

But instead of the kindness, tenderness, and love he expected to hear, she began yelling at him.

His ears were ringing so he couldn't understand what she was saying to him, but it was harsh and it was angry. All he wanted was to be held by his mama; all he wanted was a hug. Instead, he was scolded and sent to his room.

He sat on his bed once again, hoping that this was still his dream. Hoping that soon he would wake up to a mama who was kind and a father who was there. Hoping that all of this—the embarrassment on the bus, the man from the swamp, the betrayal from his mama— was a part of some extravagant nightmare that he would wake from when a little time had passed. All he had to do now was wait.

Outside, the rain still poured and the wind screamed through the tree tops as loose sticks and empty beer cans threw themselves against the house. Suddenly, there was a flash of light at the window with an explosion that rocked Lukas to the core. It sounded as if the lightning had struck right outside his window.

He sprung up to see what had happened, and that's when he saw it. That's when he saw him.

The man in blue was outside with a knowing grin—and ghoulish yellow eyes.

CHAPTER 5

BURNING LOVE

Ms. Uri counted the seconds until the school bell rang, the clock taunting her as its hands leisurely strolled around their well-beaten path—regulating, oscillating, deliberating, and hesitating.

She looked around her pottery classroom at the social experiment unfolding before her eyes—what she assumed was the government's attempt at a practical joke. Rows upon rows of restless adolescents waited in equal anticipation for the class to be over, the last barrier between them and the freedom of summer. Her students passed their yearbooks back and forth in an insincere ritual between the stereotypic archetypes. The popular kids collected in the corner, the one opposite the large kiln, downing their energy drinks and bragging to one another about what ostentatious graduation gifts they would be receiving. The geeks and nerds assembled at their workstations, schmoozing over what video games would be coming out soon and which new superhero remake would be most aligned with the comic it was originally centered upon. Others gossiped about fellow classmates and even some teachers. She listened to the bottomless barrage of meaningless dribble ceaselessly spewing from the mouths of her underlings. The valueless quibble consisted of summer plans, parties to attend, universities to apply to, celebrities to follow, where to get enough alcohol to get drunk without being carded, and which video of people hurting themselves was funniest on the Internet. Modern American-bred egocentrism at its finest.

It was a gloomy end of the school year for them. Rain poured beyond the classroom windows, but these students didn't deserve anything better.

As a child in Romania, she knew a different brand of American youth from old American reruns—Opie from *The Andy Griffith Show*, little Eddie from *The Munsters*, the *Brady Bunch* family—all of those youngsters were well behaved, courteous, and polite. They listened to their elders and obeyed the authorities over them. Once in a while they got into mischief, but their morals and character always grew from the experience. Not so with these Cretans, these inconsiderate, apathetic, cantankerous, and self-degrading imbeciles suckling from the teat of self-entitlement.

It was obvious to Ms. Uri that, in the absence of a stable father, the boys' role models were unscrupulous, womanizing celebrities. These man-children had been coached by sports stars who taught them to cheat and cut corners; musicians who illustrated that responsibilities were burdens meant to be revolted against and unchallenged adolescence was a goal worth striving for. They learned from modern television and nonstop video gaming that violence was not only pleasurable but actually entertaining to inflict upon others. The same attitudes were undoubtedly true of her ape of a husband and would likely also be passed along to her remora of a son.

The girls were no better in her mind, parented secondhand through MTV programming and Planned Parenthood commercials. They soon learned that a woman's inner loveliness was worth sacrificing on the altar of vain external beauty, that sexuality was an inconsequential tool for self-promotion or cultural advancement. Constant upgrades in social media networking reared them into self-aggrandizing narcissists whose interests extended no further than their iPhones.

The mere thought of these Philistines mating was enough to make Ms. Uri retire her humanity. Through the oval glasses that teetered on the edge of her rather large beak, she soaked up all these sights and shuddered.

Most days when she felt like this, she'd tune out her students by turning on her digital music account and letting the melodies of Buddy Holly, Jerry Lee Lewis, and her all-time favorite Elvis Presley rush over her like a soul-lifting bath, taking her to a secret place inside that no one else could enter, the place she retreated to as a child where she could be with the ones she loved. It was there where her cravings—no matter how extravagant or unusual—were catered to. Where she could spend all day feeling beautiful, desired, and pursued. This was the place she flew to in moments like this, of anticipation, anxiety, or stress.

But not today.

As much as she wanted to, she just couldn't bring herself to do it and go through the teasing again.

Although she pretended that it didn't bother her, in truth it did. It absolutely unnerved her. She knew it shouldn't, that teachers weren't supposed to allow themselves the vulnerability or opportunity of being hurt by their students.

That's why she couldn't tell anyone about it. That's why it had to be a secret.

She was afraid that if she told someone about it—anyone at all—then the teachers would ridicule her for her weakness as well. And God knew she couldn't seriously communicate with her Neanderthal husband. The mere mention of emotions was enough to drive him out of the room, and so, coincidentally, she did bring them up as frequently as possible.

For the past year or so, she had resumed the use of her maiden name, Uri, and changed her prefix back to Ms. in order to cast doubt on her marriage status. Her husband had been dead to her for years. She couldn't stand the sight of him anymore. Most nights she made him sleep on the couch, only inviting him back to bed for physical pleasure, during which time she thought only of her new special someone. She had only married him as a final alternative to being escorted out of the country when her student visa expired—a proposition he was all too happy to oblige and consummate. Nine months later, their child was born, the embodiment and continual reminder of her loveless union. Neither were of any use to her; both trapped her into the purgatorial state she had been in for the last nine years.

She was alone, a feeling she incorrectly assumed she would be used to by now.

Intellectually, she knew that she was superior to her students. That she never questioned. But she couldn't handle their backstabbing comments on social media. Her students didn't think she knew what they were saying behind her back, but she was all too familiar with their online ostracism. She had gone onto "the Facebook" and created a false account to see what her students really said about her. It was as easy as going on the Google and finding some hot pictures of "babes" to "cut and glue" as her "profile photograph." She called herself Priscilla Ann—the name of the woman who married her first crush, her true love, Elvis.

Now she had everyone fooled. She had shown them. She had shown them all. And just as she predicted, every male in her class "friend-bidden" her after she said that she was attending their high school and was looking to be in a no-strings-attached sexual relationship. After that, it wasn't long before the females requested her virtual acquaintance as well. Her plan had worked. Then she began asking what they thought about a teacher at the school named Ms. Uri.

The responses shocked her.

They referred to her not as Ms. Uri, but as Misery! Ms. Misery. They said that she looked like a vulture with her "ginormous nose," "saggin' wrinkled turkey neck," "creepin' witchy fingernails," and that her voice sounded like "she musta choked on a Russian midget." They even made fun of the music she played, calling it, "krule 'n' unusual punishment." She sobbed that evening after reading their posts.

They were all cruel—even those who had never taken a single pottery class with her.

Everyone, but one.

And that's when she saw him, her new special someone. His name was J. T., and she wasn't sure how she had missed him for the past four years. His skin was tan and firm from playing sports. His hair was dark brown and swept to one side. His interests included "hangin' out wit' my peeps," and "chillin' wit' da honeys." And, as if that wasn't enough, his eyes were blue—not a pseudo-blue from wearing colored lenses or anything, either. His eyes were liberty blue.

A God-bless-America blue. A let-freedom-ring blue.

An Elvis-Presley-the-King-of-Rock-'n'-Roll blue.

A lagoon-of-sapphire-she-wanted-to-strip-down-and-lose-her-self-in blue.

He looked just like the man she had always imagined marrying as a school girl in Romania. He looked like an angel that had stepped down from heaven to bring back purpose and passion into her life. Already, he was protecting her in a way that her husband never had. She could never forget the words of valor he spoke as he rose to extinguish the fire of her foes, "U r mean. She's not tht bad."

Oh heaven! A man equipped with wit and unparalleled communicative skills who would defend her honor against the accusations of her adversaries! Even now when she remembered it she knew that was the first time she had ever felt loved.

She pursued him through the secret messaging of the hidden pop-up talk box. Sparks flew as their conversation lasted 45 minutes, until he creatively ended the conversation with "lol g2g." And she didn't need a translator to know what he meant: "lots of love gorgeous too gorgeous." Her heart leapt. She could hardly sleep for the rest of the night or pay attention in class the next day. All she could think about was him.

She began looking for him in the halls. Anytime a figure passed her window, she would snap her head up and smile in case it was him. With every week that passed, she found herself volunteering for additional lunch-patrol duty and extra after-school activities to host in hopes of seeing him. It wasn't long before her days were filled with his presence and her nights occupied with his prose. He began asking what classes she was taking, what hobbies she enjoyed, what movies she liked to watch—questions as unfamiliar to her as being pursued felt.

He was her Romeo, her Elvis.

She shared with him some intimate aspects of her past—things not even her husband knew about. Her soul finally had a receptacle to pour itself into. Sure there were some hiccups in their relationship; some untruths here and there. But beneath the fake name, underneath the fabrications about where she grew up and how old she was, below the strategically undeclared facts about being married and having a child, and behind the phony pictures chronicling the life of a complete stranger was the same heart with the same passions and the same needs. And if it was true that love is blind, then everything else was semantics anyway. She had revealed her inner self, which to "Priscilla Ann" Uri, was the only thing that truly mattered.

Soon, the school year drew to a close and her new beau was getting impatient about meeting her. Over the past several months, they had carried on so many great conversations, agreed about so many things, shared so many intimate secrets, and were so physically attracted to one another that it only made sense for him to meet up with the "perfect girl." She was so excited to finally come face to face with her object of affection that she agreed without thinking to meet him on the last day of school in the pottery room after the school bell rang.

Now that moment had finally arrived.

Ms. Uri's heart pulsed with the clock. Each second that passed brought her that much closer to the moment in which, like the phoenix of old, she would be reborn and rise from the ashes of her miserably mundane life. The hour when she would, at last, be freed from the two confining chains that tethered her ankles to the nethermost rung of hell: the bottom-feeding fetters she referred to as husband and son.

She was excited now. She smiled, and she didn't try to hide it. She no longer cared about anything else in her life because soon, very soon, the love of her life would be there. Students were sitting on their desks, but she didn't stop them. Two of them took the bathroom pass at the same time, but she let them go. Today she was a free spirit. Today she was throwing caution to the wind.

She looked at the clock. Five minutes.

Five minutes was all she had to wait. Five minutes until he would walk through the door and rescue her from her miserable life. Five minutes and then they'd be together.

She had to find something to occupy herself—there had to be something left for her to do. She reviewed her outfit, adjusting her white scarf perfectly over her black long-sleeved blouse. She checked for lint, stains, watermarks, and clay blemishes. She made sure her manicure—sun-glow yellow nail polish from Pinky Pierce, her favorite nail salon—hadn't begun to chip. She scanned her desk for any unflattering or potentially embarrassing pictures, but she'd long ago thrown out the one of her family.

She checked the time again.

Three minutes left now.

She began tapping the desk as an outlet for nervous energy. Her favorite song, "It's Now or Never," by Elvis seemed appropriate. She hummed the tune to herself, repeating the lyrics in her head.

The words could not have rung any truer. Tomorrow would be too late for their love to take form. Her love could not wait. It had to be here; it had to be now.

One minute left. That was all that remained before he would come walking through the door. He would be there any minute now. Any minute now and he would be there, live and in person.

I think I'm going to be sick, she thought. *Maybe I should cancel— maybe I should call it off right now. What if he doesn't come? What if he doesn't like me? Oh God, what if he doesn't like me? I don't think my heart could take that, not from him.*

The bell rang.

This was it. There was no going back now.

The students threw their extra notebook paper in the air like confetti, each rushing out the door faster than the last. But she remained in her seat, silent, still, her eyes not knowing whether to fix themselves on the door or the floor, her body not knowing whether to sit or stand, her emotions begging her both to stay and to go. She was crippled with conflict.

And then, just like that, there he was. The only one rushing in as everyone else was pouring out. Blue eyes sparkling, shirt neatly pressed, each strand of his luscious locks falling precisely in place as he fought against the horde of barbarians. From the moment she saw him, her fears were quelled. This was her chance and this was her man.

Beaming, she rose to her feet. She watched her love look around the classroom in curiosity, wondering where his mystery girl was hiding. He waited until everyone had left the room before checking his watch.

No, she thought, *you're not too early. You're right on time.*

Puzzled, he walked back to the front of the room, passing Ms. Uri, in an attempt to scan the hall. Her smile only widened as he strolled on by, her insides aflutter. Working up her courage, she followed him, her black high heels applauding her every step of the way.

Now she was nearly behind him. His intoxicating blend of heavy cologne and Old Spice body wash greeted her. Feeling a presence behind him, he turned and smiled.

Her heart raced, pounding at the bars in her ribcage.

This is my moment, she thought. *This is the dream come true that I have long deserved.*

But as soon as their eyes met, his smile vanished. "I'm sorry," he said. "I thought you were someone else." And with that, he turned back to the hall where his girl would be coming through at any moment.

Didn't he know this was her? That she was his Priscilla? She cleared her throat, hoping that he would turn. He didn't. Frustrated and a bit hurt, she tapped him on the shoulder. "Excuse meh," she said in her thick Romanian accent.

"Oh, sorry." He moved out of her way, his gaze never completely acknowledging her.

"J. T., don't you know it's meh?" she asked in irritated bewilderment. He turned, his baby-blues peering into her soul. "It's meh. Preescella." At first it didn't sink in; she could see that. But soon enough it registered, and his eyes opened wide as his jaw unhinged itself slumping down to the floor.

She proceeded to confess her undying love for him, holding nothing back. She told him that he had rescued her by sticking up for her on Facebook, that she had made an account with someone else's picture to throw her students off. But she had never lied to him—not in the way it mattered anyway, and never once hid her true self from him.

She told him that he was her protector, her dream mate, her Elvis. She laid herself emotionally bare before him in unrestricted vulnerability. And now that she had given him the sensitive reinforcement she knew he needed, it was time for him to reassure her, to comfort her under the wings of his love and gently carry her away into her special place.

All she needed was to know that she was good enough.

But he laughed.

He laughed.

And not just any laugh—a belly shaking, rip-roaring, hooting and hollering, tears pooling in his eyes, couldn't catch his breath kind of laugh.

"Who put you up to this?" he managed to choke out as he panted to catch his breath. "Was it Joey? Or Ruben? It was probably both of them, wasn't it? Oh God, those guys are good." He wiped the tears from his eyes, different tears from the ones flowing down Ms. Uri's crimson cheeks. "And you! You were so incredible! For a second there, you really had me going with all the 'My husband doesn't love meh. I want you to carry meh to mine secret place.' I—I actually believed you!"

At this point, he was doubled over in a fit of laughter. Ms. Uri had never been more humiliated in her life. What had she done? Numbness and nausea commingled within her. She had been betrayed by the only person she had ever loved—the only one she had ever let get close enough to hurt her. And hurt her he did, past the point of repair. She was exposed and shamed. She was going to be sick. She reached under her desk for the wastebasket, but found only ceramic carving tools in its place. She fell on her knees. She wanted to curl up and disappear. Her knight was nothing more than a hound dog.

But then a new emotion began to emerge, an emotion she experienced rarely, but fiercely. It was coming in the name of self-preservation. It was coming to redirect the pain.

It was anger—white hot anger, bubbling over, boiling to the brim. Anger for how he had humiliated her. Anger for how he was using her pain for his entertainment. Anger for how he had led her on. Anger for how he had pursued her falsely. Anger for making her feel the way she did. Anger for the life she now knew she would never leave. She would never leave. She would never leave.

With his every laugh, she felt it growing. And he just kept laughing. Laughing at her misery. Laughing at her languishing.

Laughing uncontrollably, and she had to make it stop. She had to make it stop.

She had to make it stop!

Grabbing the carving tools that sat in place of her wastebasket, she lunged at him and thrust the rusty dull blades into the side of his throat. At first the young man was too stunned to fight back, the surprise of the stab overwhelming his senses. Finally lifting his arms to block the attack, he was met with unrelenting gouge after gouge to his hands and forearms—she exacted her revenge with the unvented force of nine years of hateful marriage. When one tool got stuck in his skin she would thrust another into him, until, slipping on his own blood, he fell to the vinyl tile floor. Over and over again she plunged the coarse, corroded knives into his face and neck, blow after blow after bloody blow until the laughing stopped—until he had apologized in blood for what he had done to her.

Then there was nothing. Then there was silence.

Coming to her senses, Ms. Uri quickly jumped off the body of her late love and checked for a pulse.

What have I done?

She couldn't remember anything. Everything had gone dark until she saw his body lying at her feet.

There was no pulse. He was dead.

Thinking quickly, she wiped her hands on a nearby hand towel and then sprinted to the door to see if there had been anybody watching. The coast was clear; no one was in the hallway. All the students had left the school as soon as the bell released them for summer.

She pulled the curtain down over her window and locked the door. She didn't have any reason to think someone would stop by to visit. The janitor didn't usually arrive until late at night, and there weren't any teachers who liked her enough to wish her well. Time seemed to be on her side. But what to do with the body?

She couldn't just leave it there lying in the middle of the room. She could say that the janitor did it, or take it out to the car and dispose of it later, but someone would probably see her lugging around a 160-pound dead student. Unless she chopped it into pieces! No, no, no. That was too disgusting to even think about. What to do?

That's when Ms. Uri turned her attention to the most important resource at her disposal—one she couldn't believe she had forgotten—the kiln. The kiln was the perfect solution to all her problems. It was in the back of her room, so she wouldn't have to lug the body anywhere; and it was large enough that she could fit the whole thing in at once, so none of that icky slice and dice mess. It was always on, so any odd smell would continue unquestioned.

The only doubt she had was whether or not it would heat up enough to cremate a body, and if it did, how long it would take. She did some calculations and figured out that the average temperature of a kiln was 2,000 degrees Fahrenheit, so it would take roughly a couple hours to bake.

That sounded good to Ms. Uri. After all, she had nowhere to be until—and that's when she remembered. She was supposed to pick her son up from school. Fortunately she had missed so many of his after-school pickups this past school year that he had been trained to go to St. Jude and wait, and nothing about this would seem out of the ordinary to any keen observer.

Confident in her course of action, she resumed her work. The only real hassle with her plan was that dragging the body to the kiln and lifting it in might prove to be a bit difficult. But Ms. Uri was a Romanian woman, and if Romanian women knew anything, it was how to do a hard day's work. Grabbing him at the ankles, she dragged him to the kiln, leaving a trail of blood and urine in his wake. She lifted him up by his underarms and, taking a parting look at her departed love, hoisted him into the furnace. Now she just had to set the timer, mop the floor, and wait until he was ready to come out.

But someone knocked at the door.

Ms. Uri sprang to attention. *Suspicious minds*, she thought.

A voice came from the other side of the door. "Mrs. Eary? Mrs.—I mean—Ms. Uri? Hi, it's Mrs. Beleaguer from across the hall. Ms. Uri?"

"Yes, hello," the flustered teacher replied. "I am just cleanink a mess one of mine students made. Can't get to the door. Is everythink okay?"

"Oh, yes, everything is fine. I just…" The door handle began to jiggle. "I was just stopping by to wish you a happy first day of summer break. Do you have a second to talk?"

"No, no. Very busy. Sorry. Have good break!"

She waited until the shadow moved from under the doorway and the sound of cheap, flat shoes drifted down the hall. *That was a close one*, she thought.

After mopping the floor, rinsing off her tools, and thoroughly covering the room in disinfectants and bleach, it was time at last to inspect. *Everything seems to be in order*, she mused in approval. Opening the access panel to the kiln, she dropped the mop head, hand towel, and her bloodstained scarf into the flames.

Now to wait.

Her eyes returned once more to the clock. There wasn't much time left now, only 15 minutes or so. Things of this nature were always hard to precisely time, but she had a feeling she had done this before. Taking a seat at her desk, she resumed tapping her sun-glow fingernails on the desk, trying not to think about the accident.

But what was she going to do with the ashes? She couldn't bring herself to leave him in there over the summer, cold and alone. He was, in spite of everything, still the love of her life. His cruel cackling sure bruised that love, but nothing could ever truly break it. He would always be in her heart, resting peacefully within the comfort of her soul. *That's it!* she thought, *resting peacefully!* She needed to make something to put his ashes in so that he could rest in peace as he deserved. A vase or urn, perhaps. She looked around at her supplies and sadly realized that she did not have enough clay to make an eternal abode for her love. Her mind was frantic; she had to give her Elvis something to rest in or he would remain restless forever.

It was then that Ms. Uri got a wonderful idea—why not mix his ashes in with the clay? If she did that, she would have more than enough material to go around. She had killed two birds with one stone, and proceeded to congratulate herself on her plan.

After a few minutes of going over all the angles of her design, she turned on her computer and played some music. Hearing Elvis Presley's "Burning Love" come on, she began to sing.

Lord Almighty,
I feel my temperature rising
Higher, higher
It's burning through to my soul
Girl, girl, girl
You gonna set me on fire
My brain is flaming
I don't know which way to go
Your kisses lift me higher
Like the sweet song of a choir

You light my morning sky
With burning love

She glanced over to the furnace where her once vibrant love now lay. "We never got that first dance, did we?" She stood and began to dance slowly as if her burning love were holding her close.

I feel my temperature rising
Help me, I'm flaming
I must be a hundred and nine
Burning, burning, burning
And nothing can cool me
I just might turn into smoke
But I feel fine
Your kisses lift me higher
Like the sweet song of a choir
You light my morning sky
With burning love

"Isn't this wonderful, J. T.? My sweet Jeremy Thomas?" she said, eyes closed, swaying sweetly with the melody as she swooned in the arms of her lover. "Our first dance." The song drew to a close.

It's coming closer
The flames are now licking my body
Won't you help me
I feel like I'm slipping away
It's hard to breathe
And my chest is a-heaving
Lord, have mercy
I'm burning a hole where I lay

It was then that the buzzer sounded. J. T. Pittas's time was officially up.

After brushing out the ashes of her love into a dustpan and mixing it into her clay, she began to mold her vase. It was a beautiful experience, a sensual experience. The soft, wet clay squeezed and squished, oozing and discharging at the touch of her fingertips. The feel of Jeremy Thomas in her hands, the smell of him in her lungs, the presence of him still lingering around her, holding her and calling out her name. She bit her bottom lip and closed her eyes as she lost herself in the romance of it all, letting her hands explore Jeremy in a way she had never before fantasized.

When the urn was finished, she cradled it as one does a newborn baby and walked it to the kiln where Jeremy Pittas's transformation would be complete. She began picturing the perfect spot for him in her home, thinking of all the experiences they would share and all the memories they would create. She imagined herself placing him on the shelf above the dinner table so that they could enjoy a candlelit dinner for two, bringing him into the bathtub late at night while sharing a glass of red wine, hiding him in the bedroom so that he could preside over her as she was sleeping.

He would be the perfect companion—never complaining, never quarrelsome, always honest, present, and loving.

Once he was done baking for the second time, she brought him out to cool. It was growing darker out now, rain tenuously tumbling to the earth. *I guess it's true what they say*, Ms. Uri thought, *time does fly when you're having fun*. When it was time to go, she reviewed the room once more before bringing Jeremy home to meet the family. Everything seemed to be in order; no evidence of his transformation had been left unattended. She then lifted up the window shade, unlocked the door, and carried her love through the evening drizzle to her parking spot at the corner of the abandoned Donn Angelos High School lot—buckling him into the front seat of her grey compact car, next to her of course.

When she got home, every light in the house was on. She walked into her son's room to check on him, to make sure he was all right.

Unlocking his door, she peered in and found him asleep. She placed her hand gently on his leg before exiting the room, closing the door on her way out. *He may be a burden, but we still love him. Don't we, J. T.?* she thought as she walked to the den.

Reaching to the second highest shelf on her bookcase, she set Jeremy down slowly and carefully. "This is your new home, my love." She kissed the palm of her hand and rested it on her most cherished possession. "This is where—"

Just then, her son came blundering into the room. "Mama! Mama!" he cried as he ran to her with open arms. But the clumsy boy slipped on the floor, lost his balance, and fell face first into the bookshelf, causing the vase to tumble out of place and nearly fall to the floor.

Pushing her son aside she lunged over to where her love was falling and caught him before his body was broken. "What is the matter with you? Don't you ever look where you are goink?" she screamed at the trembling boy, whose head began to bleed from the impact of the fall, his arms still outstretched toward her. "You are a stupid boy! A reckless, stupid boy! Go to bed!"

As her son left the room, crying, she looked down at the vase she rocked in her arms. "Everythink is okay now. Your Preescella is here." She caressed the vase.

At that moment, the front door opened, and a man wearing a mud-stained blue cloak walked inside, his every step coming closer and closer.

"And where have you been all day?" asked Ms. Uri.

"Oh—I—uh—I had some late night repair work that needed attending to," he responded as he took off his outerwear and draped it over a nearby chair.

"Well I hope you got some money this time?" She secured the vase, her eyes never leaving her love.

"I did. I made a killing," said the man with a yellow stare. The man proceeded to undress himself from his black work outfit, the one which bore the name Mr. E. "And how was your day?"

"Fine. It vas fine," she responded. "I am goink to bed now. We have a lonk drive tomorrow." She made her way to the bedroom but she stopped and turned when she reached the doorway. "I love you," she said softly.

"Yeah, love you too," responded Mr. E mechanically as he fiddled with his work shirt.

But Priscilla wasn't talking to him.

CHAPTER 6

THE VULTURES WAKE

The priest stood speechless.

From behind the cross-shaped pulpit, he gazed into his audience of two, scanning his mind for the right words to say. Seminary hadn't prepared him for something like this. After all, how was he expected to answer all the questions or comfort the many concerns that mounted in the minds of his flock when he couldn't account for them himself? Why did a good God allow good people to die? Why would a good God strip a child from the only family he had ever known? Father Michael had heard it said over and over in his training that "a priest can only lead his congregation as far into the heart of God as they themselves have traveled," but if that were true, why was this responsibility laid at his feet when he clearly wasn't ready for it?

His superiors should have known better.

It was time for him to speak now. This was when he should extend condolences to those grieving, but everything he'd written seemed like a jumbled mess of insincere clichés. "God has a reason for everything," his notes read. "There is a season for all things. Romans 8:28 tells us that 'we know that for those who love God all things work together for good, for those who are called according to his purpose.' God's ways are higher than our ways; we don't understand his greater plan. He sees the bigger picture where our eyes are limited only to the here and now. We need to walk by faith and not by sight. Let us not focus on the time that has been taken from us with our loved ones, but let us rather rejoice in the moments of love that we shared with the knowledge that we will unite with them once more—God willing—in the hereafter."

Father Michael knew that his superior was there standing in the corner, watching his every move and evaluating him on the caliber of his performance. But he didn't care. That was the least of his worries. His palms grew sweaty, perspiration collecting on his brow. Mustering the minuscule amount of courage he had left, the Father began.

"Today we gather under the banner of sorrow. We join hearts and hands in memory of the dearly departed whom we have the unfortunate business of laying to rest."

His words came out slow and methodical while still bearing the rugged marks of raw inexperience, but to Father Michael, a rocky start was better than no start at all. Looking down at the casket and urn that lay on the table before him, he continued.

"It is always a terrible thing having to bury one's parents. Unfortunately, Lukas Eary has to experience this act before God generally allows. But it is important to remember during this time of tragedy not to question what the good Lord has chosen to do, but to trust in the sovereignty of His will."

The Father took in a deep breath. He felt as if his white collar were choking him underneath his black funeral garment. Michael cringed at the thought of relaying any insincere wisdom during this time of heartache for the boy. Anything less than honest sincerity would be a mockery to the hurt and vulnerability that young Lukas was feeling.

He cleared his throat. "Is there anyone who would like to say something in memory of the loved ones who have passed?" Father Michael looked to his congregation. "Perhaps you have something to say, Lukas? Something nice to pass along about your mother or father?" The boy scribbled and scrawled in his notebook. "It could be anything, Lukas—a story, or memory would do just fine."

Lukas closed his journal and rose from his seat. He was wearing a dingy white shirt half-tucked into a pair of faded black pants. A crooked tie hung around his neck and covered his mismatched buttonholes. His loose shoe strings smacked the tile floor as he walked onto the stage. Pulling the pulpit microphone down so that he could speak into it, the boy commenced his speech.

"My mama was a good mama. I love her and miss her. I miss my daddy too. I know how much Mama liked her new vase, so that's where she is now," he said as he pointed to the cremated remains of his mother now in the urn she loved.

Then Lukas proceeded to step off stage, until Father Michael stopped him. "And what about your father, Lukas? Do you have any memories about him? Anything he liked?" the young priest asked, partially hoping to fill more time.

Lukas walked back over to the microphone. "My daddy used to take me fishing. We haven't been in a long time, but I liked it when we went fishing. He promised to take me again soon. I think he said next week we'd go."

Father Michael put his hand on the child's shoulder and crouched down low. "Son," he said, "I'm sorry that he won't be able to keep that promise to you."

The boy looked up at the priest in confusion. "But, Father, my daddy isn't dead. Just look at him."

The priest looked over at the corpse in the coffin and understood how the boy could make the mistake of thinking he was only lying down. Typically, the mortuary would glue the eyes of the departed closed, but, in the peculiar case of Mr. Eary, his haunting yellow eyes would not stay shut, unhinging themselves spontaneously. Looking into them even now, the young priest felt as if they were following his every movement, weighing his sermon and finding it wanting.

"Thank you for your words, son. You did a great job. You may be seated." Father Michael gestured the youngster back to his seat. "Is there anyone else who would like to say a word on behalf of the departed? Perhaps you, ma'am?" the priest asked, directing his question to the only other person in attendance. The Hispanic woman wore a dark purple dress with large sunglasses that covered her eyes. She appeared to be the recent victim of either an accident or abuse, with poorly concealed bruises along the edges of her face and a broken arm cast in a sling. "Would you like to say anything?" the Father asked again after waiting a moment with no response.

Before the woman could speak, a creak came from the side door of the stage. A pasty heavyset man adorned in priestly attire entered through its opening and motioned Michael over.

"Excuse me one minute," the priest said as he exited stage left. "Is there something that I can help you with, Father Tawdry?"

"How are things coming, Michael? Making progress?" the elder priest asked.

"It's going all right . . . but next time I don't want to . . . "

"That's good to hear Michael. Good to hear. Say—do you think you could wrap things up here pretty soon?"

"But Father, I—"

"It's just that we have another funeral that we've lined up to do here in a couple of minutes. I squeezed in this confirmation student and his deceased parents last minute here pro bono under the assumption that when the next funeral came, you all would be cleared out."

"But Father Tawdry, we have only just begun our service! This child deserves a good burial for his parents just like anyone else wou—"

"I understand, Michael. I really do. But these people waiting are important to the church—a family who has mourned the loss of a member who has been coming here for over 60 years! And we cannot withhold this right endowed to the partakers of the covenant on behalf of a child whose family hasn't stopped by in ages, can we? That just wouldn't sit right with the church, Michael." The elder priest looked at his younger protégé and saw a quiet frustration resting on his lips. "I'll tell you what—why don't I give you a couple more minutes in here to finish things up, give you some time to impress Bishop Unger there in the corner, and allow you to feel as though you are doing your civic responsibility to the child before we come in. I'll give you five more minutes before I come in again and dismiss." With a pat on the back, he left the lesser Father to carry out his orders.

Michael returned to the podium where the familiar feeling of speechlessness once again twisted his tongue. In a last ditch effort, the young priest flipped open his book of prayer, locating the passage that corresponded with the date, and began to speak.

"Our Scripture passage today takes us to the book of Ecclesiastes where King Solomon has written in chapter 3:16–21 this word from God: 'Moreover, I saw under the sun that in the place of justice, even there was wickedness, and in the place of righteousness, even there was wickedness. I said in my heart, God will judge the righteous and the wicked, for there is a time for every matter and for every work. I said in my heart with regard to the children of man that God is testing them that they may see that they themselves are but beasts. For what happens to the children of man and what happens to the beasts is the same; as one dies, so dies the other. They all have the same breath, and man has no advantage over the beasts, for all is vanity. All go to one place. All are from the dust, and to dust all return. Who knows whether the spirit of man goes upward and the spirit of the beast goes down into the earth?'"

The priest looked up from his text to find his audience focused in attention. Feeling renewed strength in their newfound interest, he continued, "We all have such small time on this Earth—such limited time to accomplish anything that seems to have eternal value. So much of what we live for and, many times, what we ultimately die for is measured as being infinitesimally minuscule in the grand scheme of the hereafter. After all, what is wealth when compared to eternity? Or pride, or intercourse, or vanity when looking forward to the Judgment Throne of God? So many of us live life like beasts—conscious-less, compassionless vultures, treating others like subhuman avenues through which we gain pleasure. We will all sit before God and experience judgment for the manner in which we lived our lives. The righteous who suffered on Earth will be raised up under the blood of Christ, and the wicked who prospered on this world through selfish gain will be cast low into the eternal fire. We know not where Mr. and Mrs. Eary are at this moment—but there is a way that you can have assurance about your own soul, and that is by placing your faith and hope in Jesus the Christ and living out His gospel of love on the Earth before our time is up as well."

Father Michael nodded his head in affirmation. He looked up at his congregation of two only to find Lukas etching some more writings into his journal as the mysterious woman in purple sat silently stewing in conviction. Feeling a bit disheartened, Father Michael turned his eyes to his notes and concluded the service.

"Mr. Edgar Allen Eary. Fifty-six years old. Repairman by trade. We pray for your soul. Mrs. Ginger Alden "Uri" Eary. Forty-four years old. Schoolteacher by trade. We pray for your soul. Now in the words of the Aaronic Benediction, 'May the Lord bless you and keep you; may He cause his spirit to shine on you and be gracious to you; May He lift up His smile on you and give you peace.'"

With those final words of blessing, the service was over. An organ began to play softy in the background as the priest left the stage and walked briskly out the back door to the sanctuary, head hung low, his superior following close behind.

The woman in purple watched from her position on the pew as the child, who sat a few rows ahead of her, rose from his seat and walked over to the coffin of his father. She listened as the boy talked to his dad as if nothing had happened, as if death had never slipped its icy hand between them in separation. The child spoke so tenderly and lovingly to his deceased father that she couldn't help but think about her own son and how sweetly he spoke to her at such an age. She missed him so much now. It had been six days since she had last seen him, her Jeremy.

Her mind couldn't help but to reminisce about the wonderful times they shared and, God willing, the wonderful times they would share again. And little Lukas reminded her so much of her sweet boy—the way he spoke, acted, and loved. She could tell from just hearing him speak that he had a big heart—one that needed a mother's love. But she had taken that love away in her recklessness and irresponsibility. She had not been able to sleep the last few days because of what she had done, and, of course, because of her Jeremy missing.

She wished there was something that she could do for the boy. She wished she could help ease his pain.

She wished until she realized that she could help the lad, and in so doing she might even be able to ease her pain too. What if she adopted the boy? He needed a mother, and she needed a son. What if she brought him into her family? It would be an act of contrition—an atoning for past sins rendered.

She would be as good a mother as any.

The woman got up from her seat and headed over to the child. "Excuse me," she said as she rested her hand gently on his shoulder.

Lukas turned to her. "Hello, you don't know me, but my name is Ms. Pittas and I . . . well, I knew your mother and father, and I was wondering if you have any plans for lunch today? If you don't, then I would love to get you something to eat! You know, help take care of you a bit with your parents gone and everything. How does that sound, Lukas?"

The boy smiled, his dark rimmed glasses rising with the elevation of his ears. Ms. Pittas extended her hand to the boy, his small palm dwarfed in her loving tender touch, and the two began to exit the sanctuary.

The next funeral began its procession as the new mother-and-son team were walking out the door, the influx of attendees forming an unintentional blockade for the couple. A woman with blonde hair and green eyes sat in the plush crimson chair that rested just outside the doors to the sanctuary, her body on the edge of the seat with one hand on her forehead and the other holding up her cell phone.

Being stuck in place, Ms. Pittas couldn't help but to overhear the conversation.

"What do you mean you can't find him?" the woman asked angrily over the phone. "Officer—what do you mean you just can't find him? My brother would not just bail out on our father's funeral. Can you check again, please? Yes, his name is Russell—no, no not Russell Dearly. Dearly was our father's last name. No, he changed it to our mother's maiden name of Prey. Uh-huh. That's correct. P-r-e-y . . . yes . . . thank you. Please keep looking for him—I really need him to be here right now. I'm afraid something is wrong. I just have a gut-feeling that something awful has happened. Yes. Yes, thank you, officer."

Being momentarily halted from their afternoon lunch date, Ms. Pittas initiated a light conversation with her child. "So, Lukas," she started, "how are you coping with all the different changes going on? I bet it's been a rough week for you to handle."

"I dunno. What do you mean?" he replied inquisitively.

"Well, you know, with your mom and dad passing away? I know that must be tough on you not having a mother."

"Oh, yeah. Mama is gone, and that's sad for me. But my daddy's not gone. He's only lying down." He smiled as if to reassure her.

"Only lying down, Lukas?" she asked.

"Uh huh. And pretty soon he is going to get up and take me to go fishing down at the marsh."

"Lukas, sweetie. I hate to be the one to tell you this, but your daddy is gone, honey." Ms. Pittas rubbed his back.

"Nah huh! If my daddy is gone, then why are his eyes open?" Lukas asked as he turned around and pointed to the coffin.

Ms. Pittas looked in horror as two hell fire eyes peered out of the casket and slowly turned to her, glaring unflinchingly into her spotted soul, reminding her of the unspeakable secret they shared together and of the eternal place he would soon welcome her into.

www.ingramcontent.com/pod-product-compliance
Lightning Source LLC
Chambersburg PA
CBHW060355180626
46817CB00008B/3029